eyeballs growing all over me

. . . again

eyeballs growing all over me . . . again

tony rauch

ERASERHEAD PRESS
PORTLAND, OR

ERASERHEAD PRESS
205 NE BRYANT STREET
PORTLAND, OR 97211

WWW.ERASERHEADPRESS.COM

ISBN: 1-936383-33-0

The author would like to thank the following for their assistance, support, and/or encouragement in assembling this collection: John Colborn, Sarah Fox, Margret Rauch, Dan Noyes, Lexi Johnson, Stacey Johnson, Carlton Mellick, Rose O'Keefe, Tom Dahlstrom, Lauren Bartel, Spout Press, Eraserhead Press, Whistling Shade Press, and Joel Van Valin.

". . . in stressing personal freedom as man's basic reason for being. And personal freedom meant liberation from all the cultural hang-ups imposed by authoritarians, all the societal structures that deny truth and create walls between us all."

- Anthony Scaduto

"Knowing that the testing of your faith produces patience. But let patience have its perfect work, that you may be perfect and complete, lacking nothing."

- James 1: 3, 4

". . . we also glory in tribulations, knowing that tribulation produces perseverance; and perseverance, character; and character, hope. Now hope does not disappoint, because the love of God has been poured out in our hearts by the Holy Spirit who was given to us."

- Romans 5:3, 5

"Blessed are the merciful, for they will be shown mercy."

- Matthew 5:7

Contents

i. tomorrow, through the portal

ii. i found them in the weeds

iii. now we can buy a monkey

tomorrow, through the portal

the stench

I come home, step inside, set my briefcase on the floor, lift off my hat, draw in a breath—and that's when it hits me. Wwwoooooffff. I draw in a stinging, mossy smell I have never before encountered. It is a thick, pungent, stagnant lake, sweaty gorilla kind of tangy, swirling fog of rotting vegetables stench. "Whoa, boy," I cough. "What in the name of Mother Goose is that?" I gag.

My wife steps from the hall and gestures in a neighborly manner, as if to present a new guest. She puts her other finger up to her mouth in the international "Ssssshhhh" symbol. She is wearing some type of inhaler mask—something she must've gotten from a storage locker out in the garage—from when the painters were here—some type of yellow, cheap, strap—on, plastic de—stenching device. I shrug and hold up my palms in the "What gives?" pose. She points, poking her hand at the couch and furrows her brow at me.

I turn my head to where she's pointing. Sitting there on our couch watching t.v. is a great big hairy beast. He is huge —eight feet tall at least. His thick, shaggy brown hair is matted and snarled. And the stink. Worst stench ever. A crippling fog. "Oh, man," I mouth, bending at the knees dramatically. "Where did that come from?" I cover my nose with my hand.

My wife shrugs, "Just wandered into the house. I think it was warm," her voice is muffled behind the breathing apparatus. "You know how hot it's been." Her voice is a strange whistling wheeze.

The beast turns its big shaggy brown head to look at me.

Whatever it is, it's an ugly mother, that's for sure. I stand and nod to it in a friendly greeting, then tilt my head to look at it one way, and then another. I step forward, hang my hat on the top of the coatrack without looking, and walk across the living room and sit down on the couch, settling in next to the brown, raggy beast. I look him over. Gnats buzz about him. He holds a glass of water on his leg. At first glance, in proportion to him, it looks like a glass of water, but it's actually an entire plastic pitcher of water.

I nod and smile. The beast gazes down on me blankly, then turns his head back to the t.v. before us. A wilderness movie is showing—forests and mountains and streams and meadows and bears and everything, just as this area used to be before we rode the glaciating wave of sprawl out to cover it all.

After a while I nod. "Yeah," I exhale heavily. "It's been hot." But the beast doesn't say anything, doesn't even move. "Really hot."

Later in bed, my wife and I argue quietly. "We can't let 'im stay here," I whisper from behind my plastic breathing mask. "We can't live like this." My whisper is nothing more than a thin, distant, tinny muffle. Even though it was lying on the cool cool concrete floor of the basement laundry room, in the crisp coolness of air conditioning, I could still taste its sharp, stinging odor. We even put pillows up against the duct grills along the floor so as to not have the air conditioning draw up its crippling soupy fog of stench.

"Maybe we could cut its hair, give it a bath, hose it down?" my wife whispers from the breathing mechanism. "Soap it up?"

After a while, I just can't take it anymore. "I'll get the scissors," I roll over and drop my feet to the floor.

"Yep," my wife rolls out of bed too. "There's gotta be a solution to every problem," she shakes her head, the mask shaking in the darkness. "There's just gotta be."

We creep downstairs, tiptoeing, slowly peeking around the corner of the paneling. But it is gone. The beast has left. I step out from around the corner.

I feel weird now, disappointed. Sad. Sad that I have let it down—that I was given this chance, an opportunity to contribute and help someone out, and here I let it slip right through my fingers. Here I let it down.

I look around. The basement seems so very empty now. So lonely and ashamed in its emptiness.

My wife stands behind me. "Well, it's much cooler out now," she sighs, holding the big scissors.

And I picture him now, prowling the neighborhood, lurching down the empty streets, lurking in the shadows, heavy gaited, hunched, dragging itself in a sideways lope, thick matted hair, looking for an open door or window, looking for a nice, friendly couple. Looking for nice people, for better people. For people not like us.

I turn to my wife. "Honey, let's have children," I exhale and nod desperately. "Lots and lots of children."

I discover an army of . . .

There is a very nondescript house down the block. The old Oppalla place. 100% average. All but invisible in its conformity. And that fact fascinates me. I think about it often as I walk. I am the paper boy for this neighborhood, you see; so in a sense, I too am invisible—just a banal fixture—like the lamp posts and mail carrier and sanitation workers. And in being around so much, I am able to pick up on things the average person would not, as I can now view past what is there, seeing through mere appearances. I have open access. I am all around—here, there, and everywhere. I possess an open vision into unconscious mental processes, latent or manifest conflicts, insights into reasoning matrixes, memory, motivations gone astray, psychologies gone haywire, skewed philosophies, religions in need of adjustments, beliefs gone wrong, and so on.

I can tell you, for example, that the house right over there—the gray one, that's Lazy Pete's. He has been busy sending out a dense, 3,253 page novel he has been pecking away at. He sends it out one telegram at a time, about half a page each telegram lest someone else attempts to sabotage his efforts. The next house, that one over there, the Wilson's, has only Mr. Wilson left in it. He spends his days riding the city buses, just riding around and around. It's his hobby—says he meets the nicest people, the most interesting folks. Then there's the Blonkstoublers—disoriented, rumpled, disheveled, in need of saving, but who has the time? Then the Glonkshloppers, in disbelief, confused, timid, not knowing what to do, hiding away, missing out on so much, entire days spent peeking out from behind closed curtains. And then Ms. Flamboucher, a baroness, obsessed with perfecting her marmalade. But I don't see what the big deal is. I mean, marmalade is marmalade, after all. And then the Xiphosura's, their refusal to compromise in any way, so continuous as to move me. Their refusal to wear clothing, their refusal to bathe, their "back—to—nature" vibe. Then Mr. Dreisel, so particular that he divorced his wife because he didn't like the way she sneezed. They tried everything, including medical procedures the likes of which I can not bring myself to describe. She finally had to go, and then she was gone, and then, later on, after all that, for some reason, he cut down all the trees in his yard. It's barren now. Blank. Hey, he's a man who knows what he wants. Yes, in being around so much, I see many things, but I swear, I never saw this coming. . . I guess my curiosity just ended up getting the better of me. . .

Walking around by myself all afternoon provides me time for solitude and introspection, time to observe and think, time alone with my thoughts, time to reason and consider. I'm not out wasting time trying to formulate excuses as to exactly why and how I am so so so much better than everyone else, like so many of my insecure, paranoid, hate—filled peers seem to be doing. No, I'm not out burning time, marking time, flipping coins, hanging out, just existing. No, I want to do something with my life. I want to be something. I don't want to be a layabout, a phony, a poser. Me, I'm a curious one, more and more as time wears on, my curiosity a burning itch I'm unable to scratch, like an infection burrowing deeper into my consciousness until it becomes a part of me, a parallel existence, a manifest state of being. I'm not a doer, a fixer, or a maker. And I'm not a talker, thank God. No, I am a studier, an observer, a plotter. And I walk on. Luminous pink and gray clouds glow and whirl in the dusk on the horizon. A thin, lavender line appears like a skin forming on a cooling pot of pudding. The sun is setting, and I've decided that I am ready to make my move. The time is ripe. The time is now.

From hanging around the neighborhood, I've picked up on the general movements of the area, people's habits, comings and goings, vibes, textures, undercurrents, and so forth. And I can tell you from experience that the old Oppalla place has a suspicious new owner, especially when compared to the other people around here. Or maybe it's just that bland, boring rambler style house that makes everything around it seem more than it really is. Maybe it's just the contrast of the banal with the suspicious that sparks an interesting reaction. I don't know. But I do know that the new guy is a scientific man; you can tell just by looking at him. Plus, I've sneaked peeks at his mail and garbage. Many times. For I have been studying him. I even peer in his windows at night on a regular basis. Yeah, that new guy is smart, calculating, keeps to himself. Yeah, he's up to something, that's for sure. And since everyone else is too busy to notice, I guess it's up to me to uncover his plans and expose them to the world. It's my duty. Plus there's nothing else to do in this pathetic suburb of dullards, the mundane, the average, the unimaginative.

I've been taking notes. His first name is Ambrose. He has a number of mysterious and suspicious visitors. He gets a lot of packages delivered to his house. Big packages. Mysterious and suspicious packages. He has strange refuse in his garbage cans. Strange refuse. He stays at home most of the day. He only goes out at night. And when he is out, he stays out for long stretches. I'd like to follow him, but I am not allowed to drive. I'm not old enough. I'm only a kid. But I've been studying his patterns for weeks—a little hobby of mine, a pass time, a curiosity, an itch. And now the time is right. Tonight is the night. I have it all planned out. I make my move under the cover of darkness. Stealthily I slide out from under my blankets and slip like a piece of paper through the crack in my window. I'm in my darkest pajamas. I crouch in the bushes below my window, in the shadows of the bushes and trees, in the shadows of the house. Stealth. Deadly, clinical stealth. Slowly I crawl, close to the dark ground, from shadow to shadow, from bush to bush. I creep quietly, stopping to hide and listen—to see if anyone is following, listening, lurking.

I've been reading a lot lately, studying. I've been reading about burglary and locksmithing, camouflage and magician's tricks. I've been practicing card tricks and pick—pocketing to perfect my slight—of—hand. That sort of stuff. And so, I wait till he leaves, lying flat in the darkness, hidden under layers of leaves. I carefully creep up and quietly unhook a panel in his air conditioning system and wiggle my way in. I have been studying the system and its components for weeks. Once inside the cooling system, I immediately tumble into the family room. I need to make my way to the basement. That's where I figure Ambrose and his hoard are cookin' up their chemical goo. Yeah, they're probably up to no good. And I feel it's my duty to expose them.

The family room is sparse and boring. The place is virtually empty. There is nothing in it other than a stack of newspapers in one corner and some mason jars lined up along one wall. I creep over to the jars, quietly crawling on my stomach. I look inside, only to find some thick, golden liquid with strange milky things floating around inside. I swear they almost look like little embryos forming.

I crawl away, on my way to the basement. The darkness inside is a sketchy, charcoal gray—so strange and uneventful as to be a curiosity. The place looks like the economical stage set of a community theater. There is a chair in a far off corner, but none around the kitchen table. There are a couple of boxes stacked in another corner, and a sleeping bag in another room, but no real furniture beyond that.

Eerie lights emanate from a crack in a closed door. I slink over. It is a dull green. The light kind of flickers, as if oozing up from under deep, cloudy water. Carefully, I pull myself over, stopping every few seconds to listen to the blank night. All is quiet, so slowly I pull back the door. The hinges squeak. I slither my way into a green, fog—like haze, slowly sliding down the stairs, inching my way along on my belly. I hold my breath in anticipation, sliding one careful step at a time. Once down the stair, I listen to see if anyone is around. All is quiet, so slowly I straighten up to stand. I stand there listening some more in the thick green mist of light. Eventually I pick up a strange, faint bubbling noise and a series of funny dripping sounds. I can't quite make out as to where they are coming from. Maybe he has drippy plumbing or a refrigerator down here. Or maybe he has some exotic fish tanks or something.

I take a few steps in the blinding darkness, my eyes beginning to adjust to the weird, faint green glow. The basement is sparse too, but slowly tanks come into view. Maybe I'm right, maybe he collects rare fish, or maybe he's cooking up a bad batch of harmful chemicals. As my eyes adjust to the cloudy green glow, tanks come into view, row after row of big, long fish tanks, stacked one atop another up to the ceiling. I slowly step to one of the aquariums. Other—worldly bubbles project out of the tanks, refract onto the ceiling and floor, and split me into a hundred shadows, each one more weak and transparent than the last.

I shuffle over to the closest tank—one slow, careful, quiet step at a time. The basement is cool and dank; my hands quivering in curiosity in the chill. My breath exhales little puffs of mist. I lean to look into the tank, but cannot see anything through the condensation dripping down its surface and the faint glow pulsating from within.

I'm in front of the last series of tanks which run down the long wall of the basement before the stair. More tanks fill out the middle of the room, tons of them stacked in crisp, neat rows, one atop another. Next to me are a workbench and several chalkboards. The chalkboards are full of scribbled writing—stuff about dark matter, dense matter, condensed matter, bioinformatics, bio—analytical chemistry, pharmacokinetics, plant pathology, high energy theory, neutrino physics, neutron scattering, gravitational lenses, and gravity waves.

The workbench appears to be full of laboratory equipment—beakers and a city of test tubes. It is clean and tidy, very organized. I lean in and study a petri dish in front of me. Floating inside is a transparent little thingy—like a baby tadpole in a milky substance. As I gaze in on it, the transparent little thing turns over.

I jump back in sick horror as the little tadpole person rolls and squirms. It looks like a forming human baby—a zygote or embryo—a small tiny little wee person, not fully constituted just yet, not blown up to a recognizable scale or proportion. My head jolts back, away from the strange little thing. Who are these people to be practicing such modern witchcraft? I turn and creep over to one of the aquariums. The infinite night outside seems empty and remote. Just then I think I hear something—maybe a car pulling up or a dog running past outside. Maybe some kids playing hide—and—seek. I stop in my tracks and listen, but there is nothing. Then I lean closer, peering inside, but it is all just cloudy, milky goo with strings of creamy thick gunk—light green shimmering through from the light on the other side of the tank. And then, through the foggy clouds and bubbles, something floats into view.

My eyes adjust and focus better and I begin to make them out, strange shapes and shadows becoming more clearly defined, more recognizable through the ghostly green haze. I start to recognize the thick, dark, heavy shapes in the cloudy liquid. They are people! Tiny people! Fragile and doll—like, loose and gooey, less transparent than the really tiny one in the petri dish, but still mostly see through. They are the size of large dolls, fully proportional to a regular person. Several more dark shapes appear floating in the soupy goo. There they are—tank after tank—an army of clones growing in my neighbor's basement! I gasp at the thought and stagger back a step. My knees buckle and shiver. Finally, I bend at the waist, doubling over, sickened, but still I can't turn away. I shake my head, and just then one of the tank people floats into the side of the tank, bumping up against the glass. It just hangs there bobbing in the juice for a second. Then, slowly, gradually, it opens its eyes. It looks right at me!!

I jump back and cough a muffled screech of horror, "Aaahhh", I exhale. And the strange little thing reaches out an arm to me, touching the glass with its tiny palm. And then I recognize it. My God! It's me! It's me! They all are! An army of clones! Secret clones. An entire army. Miniature replicas of me. An army of me. I fall back in horror. My legs go numb again and I crouch in weakness, gasping for breath. I wonder if there are other houses like this around the neighborhood. Maybe . . maybe every house is like this.

I've got to get out of here. I've got to tell someone, call the authorities, warn everyone. But what if they're all in on it too? I've got to do something. But who can I trust? I've got to move, get out of here. I turn for the stair, and just then I hear the door upstairs burst open. A man runs down the stair in the darkness. I don't recognize him because it is so difficult to see in this weird light. He's nothing more than a vague, gray outline.

The man stops at the bottom of the steps and looks at me. He turns his head to the upstairs and yells: "Hurry! One of them is loose!"

I can't move. I can't even feel anything. The man steps to me, smiling. "It worked. It worked," he repeats to himself, still smiling and looking right at me, right into my eyes.

"Get 'im back in the tank!" someone rushes down the steps. It is Ambrose. He turns and stops at the bottom of the stair. He looks at me with a serious glare, in his serious clothes, his serious hair, his serious straight mouth, his serious lean frame.

I'm so afraid I can't move or feel anything. This numbing

sensation only grows worse. It's like I'm solid and heavy, made of cement or filled with sand.

Ambrose walks to the man in front of me. "That one," he begins, "that one there is not from the tanks," he gestures. "I mean look, he's fully clothed."

"Wha . . what are you . . ." I stammer. "I . . . I . ."

"It's o.k.," Ambrose raises his hand out to me in friendship. "We know you mean us no harm. Please believe me, we need you. We need your help. Please. Please trust us."

"Commander," the other man whispers, "we must protect the brigade at all costs."

"Yes, yes I know," Ambrose nods, "but we need his help in doing so." He directs his attention to me. "We need your help, son. We are not from around here. We are being invaded. . . By a . . . well, it's all just to . . . It's . . . It's just so horrible. We . . . It's very difficult to explain. It all started very very long ago. . . It's a . . ." His expression grows less serious, more loose and friendly, more hopeful, but in an exasperated plea, "We just need . . .We need your help—a place to hide. To protect our future. To plan . . . a counter offensive. . . Will you please, please help us? . . Please? . . You're our last chance. . . Our only hope of survival."

"I suppose," I look around and sigh, ". . . I will help you. . . But first . . . First you've got to do something for me. . ."

"Yes. Anything," Ambrose nods.

"I . . . I need a mini—bike."

gigantic

A man is tucked snuggly in bed at night, comfortable and warm, rushing along the soft currents of sleep. He dreams he's being watched, a cloudy vision of some giant something looking in on him, a large eye peering in to cover the entire window.

Suddenly a fantastic ripping cuts the serene silence of morning. A jagged roar crushes the soft air for just a moment. The sudden, rough tearing jostles the man awake. He snaps up in bed screaming, "Ahhh aahhhggghhh."

His wife is sleeping next to him. She rolls over and grabs him, trying to calm him, trying to pull him back down, back down into sleep. Finally she has to sit up and squeeze his arm. "What is it? What is it? What is it Honey?" They are both breathing hard by this time in the quiet darkness. Their eyes adjust to the unexpected morning light, and they feel an invading coolness all around, smell the fresh new morning air, a peach light forming to illuminate their world, their bedroom.

They feel a slight breeze. A sharp chirp from a bird cracks the fresh air. They look around and see the sky, the hazy green distance, the leaves and branches of the trees close to the house. He grabs her and pulls her close. The roof is missing. It is gone, completely gone. Shards of tarpaper, shingles, and bits of plank flap in the breeze about three feet from the floor all around their bedroom. Everything is illuminated in an odd, misty morning peach kind of tone.

They continue to examine their surroundings—random shingles on the floor, shingles on their bed, jagged, bent, twisted wood hanging just above the floor. They turn to notice a hulking beast loping away. They sit up and turn around for the thing is behind them now. They stand up on to their knees, holding onto the back of the headboard, leaning over the ragged edge of their upstairs to catch the giant, gleaming, metallic robot who has been watching them. The silver robot is lumbering away, hulking twenty feet above the tree line, stepping carefully through each yard, respectfully avoiding a clothesline, a dog house, a car in a driveway—careful not to disturb a garden, a bicycle, a tool shed. In its metal clutch they spot a grip of twisted rafters and wood framing, as if holding crunched toothpicks. Random scraps of wood and shingles form a line in the yards to where the giant is standing. "Aw," the woman sighs, "I think he's lonely."

Then they see, as the beast sinks over the tree line, a strange black Cadillac sitting down the block. The long gleaming car slowly starts up the street to pass their house. One of its windows is cracked, with an antennae sticking out of it as if from one of those radio remote control devices. The woman looks at her husband and shrugs and sighs, "I wonder if that's little Freddie? . . . she gasps, "Could it be?"

"I always wondered where he ran off to," the man shakes his head. "After all these years, I still wonder if we'll ever see him again, if he'll ever come back to us, if he'll ever return."

They sit there on their bed, in the crisp morning air, and watch the long black limousine disappear around the corner to follow the great gleaming silver robot out of sight.

"He never did like us much, did he?" the man exhales wistfully.

"Maybe. Maybe not back then," the woman shrugs, the corner of her mouth moving, almost forming into a slight little hopeful smile, "But maybe now he misses us."

send krupac through the portal

Desmond has this wild idea about how I can win Margo back. You see she is the love of my life—my everything—and I haven't been the same since she left me. I haven't been able to eat or sleep or perform even the most basic tasks without sliding into a pronounced stupor. I spend my days just staring off into space in disbelief, thinking of her, thinking about the life we could've shared together. She was my entire world, but it all came to an end a month ago. It's as if everything I've ever wanted has been erased. And all that is left is this blank, windy void that I now live in. I can't ever remember feeling this desperate or dark or empty or hopeless. My entire life has gone to ruin. There's nothing left waiting for me but a forever of bare, cold wind and this desert of a life, this wasteland that I wander through, light and empty inside, moping through vast empty void after vast empty void.

I try and try to get her back, but nothing seems to sway her heart. I try wooing her with flowers, but they only give her a rash. And the little bugs on them end up killing her cat. I send her a fantastically long love letter. But it gets put in the wrong mailbox and some big guy comes over and roughs me up, thinking that I'm after his wife or daughter.

I try everything in the book. And for the most part Margo puts up with it politely, telling me that maybe in another time, another place, we were meant to be together, but she just doesn't feel it here and now. Not now. She just needs time, she says. Maybe in a little while. Maybe in the future. Maybe.

But I just can't function. For I have looked into the face of love and had it look back at me and whisper my name. My name. And now fate has left me a ghost without her—nonexistent, unwhole, a foggy, amorphous mist. Something has let me down. Something has broken. Something has worn out. Destiny, chance, the cosmos, life, luck, kismet, karma, myself. And now all I am sure of is that I can't live like this. I spend my days in the dark, listening to old records—mostly teen tragedy tunes from the 50s and 60s, romantic slow dance numbers, the occasional sad folk ballad, some country and western, and lots of traditional Appalachian folk songs—mostly the ones about coal mine disasters and ladies in waiting. I hang my head. I mope. I spend hours alone in the darkness, haunted by the specter of failure. For I have joined the darkness, and we have become one. Nothing seems to be able to pull me from this biting pit of lost hope. Something needs to be done.

My friends attempt to drag me from my misery, to alleviate my heartache. They take me out—Spider and Philson and Rasa and Luke and Ford—to dinner, movies, clubs, and ball games, but nothing seems to cheer me up. Desmond can't watch me turn into this shriveled onion of a person, my imagination aching, my faith stretched beyond comprehension. Perhaps I should give up, detach my old dreams so that maybe new ones might grow in their place. Perhaps it is not meant to be. Like she explained: Not here. Not now. Maybe in another place, another time, another life.

My friends lend counsel and advice; however, nothing seems to take hold, nothing seems to make me feel better until Desmond finally mentions he may have a solution, one last gasp effort, although it would require drastic measures on my part. He has grown weary of my pathetic moping and claims to fear the boundaries of my stupidity. I am intrigued and listen while he explains the situation. You see he has been working in this lab. Desmond has acute insomnia. I mean the guy rarely sleeps at all, so he works a few nights a week here and there for a cleaning company. It's extra money for him, and something for him to do in the middle of the night while he's wide awake. It's something to force him to get out of the house and interact instead of flipping the channels late at night from one Gomer Pyle rerun to another. It's a quiet, mellow gig. Anyway, the cleaning company has a contract to tidy up an office of this government lab in the basement of an old Air Force base at the edge of town. He has worked for this client for over a year and a half and has gotten to know the guys who are stranded there on the night shift pretty well. There's only a few people on the late late shift and they get incredibly bored and lonely working deep into the foggy depths of night, so they're grateful for any company at all. Gradually, over the days and months and plunging into the further reaches of night, Desmond has gained their friendship and trust. He brings them doughnuts some nights or a few odd beers another, or just listens to their problems, or chats about sports or current events as he sweeps and mops and cleans. Until one day he inquires as to why they are here. Gradually they open up and tell him about their jobs.

It seems the government, during its various researches into experimental technologies, has stumbled upon some pretty interesting stuff. For example, one time back in the 40s they were working on ways to camouflage their ships by sending out radio waves to cloak them from enemy radar. It seems the radio waves, when concentrated and tuned to certain frequencies in certain strengths, actually ended up rendering the ships invisible by sending them into another time—stream. It seems they just jumped into the next timeline, as if these magnetic radio waves opened a door to a room next to this one that you could just step right into. Poof. You're gone. Just like that.

The government fiddled around with these radio waves, hoping to hide things from our enemies, or hoping to transport large objects instantaneously from one part of the globe to another—ships and planes and tanks and stuff—but they couldn't get it right. They told Desmond that the metal became too hot or unstable or something. They could only send them into a parallel time—field, but not to another part of this world. They found that they were able to hide stuff in certain timelines though. It seems that our universe has several time—streams running side—by—side, bundled together and heading in the same direction at the same speed, and that we can access these various time—streams by creating electromagnetic portals that can distort time. All you need to do is generate enough of the right kind of magnetic energy, concentrate it, and you can slow down time just a little and hold it in place for just a moment, just long enough to get a doorway to form that you can walk through, and you'll be in a world similar to ours, a world right next door.

Desmond tells me that they explained to him that each of these worlds are just like our own, only slightly different. So in one time—stream I am an architect because I have an interest in architecture. In another time—stream I am a writer because I have a natural inclination toward the written word. In another I'm a banker because I think banks are interesting. And so on. Anyway, apparently we are all the same people and have similar, but slightly different, lives in each of these separate time—fields. So if you're 23 year old in this life, then you're 23 in all the others and so on because they are similar worlds, bound together somehow. But your life is just slightly different in each, as if you've chosen different options or have had other opportunities that guided your path in life. For example, you may be married in one timeline, but single in another. You may own a house in one world and live in an apartment in another. In one you're rich, in another you're poor. But you're the same person. These lives are merely mathematical possibilities of what could happen given certain sets of circumstances mixing together. Anyway, the government feels there are 23 different time—streams that they can access. Maybe there are more, maybe even an infinite number, but the 23 are all they've located and identified to date based on tuning in to specific frequencies of concentrated energy, radio waves, magnetism, and such.

Even more interesting is the idea that there may be even more worlds beyond the ones they've found to date. Apparently these bored, late night scientists have been doing research on their own and feel it might be possible to tune into even more similar worlds and times, only these new ones would be progressively more and more different than our lives here in this one. If they can tune in far enough out from the ones they've already found, they hope to find some dimensions that are as of yet barely inhabited or developed. So think of this world, only in, say the year 1750 or 1420 or something. They think that maybe they could eventually explore and settle in them. So if and when we run out of room in this dimension, we can simply spread to some other ones that are less crowded. And they postulate that there may be even more dimensions buried within all the others. So that each independent world may have access to many others. They are not other dimensions, or other worlds, or different plains of existence, they're just like here, only each has its own slight variations based on various logical probabilities. So that notion has Desmond thinking that it is very possible that Margo is single in one of these other lifelines.

Desmond sat on this information for a long time. Then he got the idea to send me into another time—field to find Margo and win her over in that space and time as I'm getting nowhere with her in this one. He's thinking maybe the lab guys can zip me into another time—stream one of these nights and maybe I can find a Margo that is interested in starting a relationship with me there. She might not even know me at all in one of those other timelines as our paths may not have crossed due to various arbitrary factors that would've kept us apart.

So Desmond explains all of this to me and I accept the challenge, and now we're on our way to his work. His friends in the government are willing to help me. In the name of true love they are going to sneak me through their electromagnetic radio wave portal and into the next time—stream, and I'll try to find her and win her hand all over again.

Me, I'm up for it! I'm so excited! I'm not one to cut and run. No. I'm a fighter, I tackle things head on, dive in, get it done. I can't wait. I pack a bag and am on my way. I figure I could just sit here and wait for her to return, which isn't very likely at this point, or I can go and find her. If not here, then maybe in another lifetime. I feel her waiting out there for me, in one of them, in a life we were meant to share.

We pull up to the lab. It is amazingly late at night. The entire planet is impressively silent, like a shiny black void. They sneak me in. Desmond hides me in his large trash can on wheels. They roll me down long hallways with surveillance cameras until we enter the room. They lift me out and show me the place—a huge underground warehouse with bare white walls and bare white floors and a bare white ceiling and a little control panel protected behind glass in a tiny control room. The place is stunningly banal and unimpressive.

There are only two men in lab coats. They approach us and explain it all to me—that they can actually monitor me and pull me back at any time as long as I have a special electrical monitor with me at all times. Basically, it is a walkie—talkie tuned to a specific frequency that they can reach to locate me. They hand it to me. It is the size of a pager and I slip it into my pocket. But they can not promise me that Margo will fall for me in the next time—stream, but that, if I'm up for it, we can always try another. I agree and thank them profusely for their assistance.

And they go on to promise that they won't send me to any of the wrong time—streams. And I'm all like whoa—whoa— whoa, what wrong time—streams. And they explain about how our government in this world has fought wars in other time— streams—old wars and new wars, secret wars and famous wars. They tell me of one time—stream that became invaded by bug—like aliens. So they sent in some neutron bomb thing that wiped everyone out—the bugs and, unfortunately, all the people there too. Now they're just waiting for the dust to settle so they can repopulate it with people from other timelines. It's like they set off a giant roach bomb in there to fumigate the place and exterminate all the bugs, and now they're just waiting for the toxins to dissipate.

They have also sent advanced scouts and agents into each time—stream to monitor activity, to see if there's anything useful to us going on. The agents check in from time to time. We can only assume that each independent dimension has done the same. But that was many years ago, they say. The portal project has fallen out of favor for reasons never expressed. The government just sent orders to shut it down one day. They were never told why. The project and all the equipment have basically been in mothballs for years. They only keep a skeleton crew here at the site, just a custodial staff of technicians—just in case they need to reactivate the electromagnetic field for some reason. Just in case they need to re—open one of the portals.

They test the equipment from time to time, starting it up and shutting it down. Tuning it to the different frequencies, tuning in different time—fields, contacting the other agents in them, recruiting more agents and spies. Occasionally they practice by sending stray dogs into other time—streams, to make sure the current can still handle complex biological organisms. So they're just using this as a test—using me, but not telling their bosses on their report. They're just going to say they were performing a routine test and have sent in another dog.

They say they don't have much to do at night, so they fiddled around until they located a dimension where I don't exist and she is presumed single, or unmarried at least. "I don't exist?" I shrug. "Not anymore," they say, "You passed in a sledding accident." "That's right," I gasp, "I hit a tree when I was nine. I was hospitalized . . ." "Yes, in this time—stream you made it. But in that one you passed. So if you show up later, with a new name, nobody will know the difference. It'll be like you're new in town. You moved there from far away." "Yeah, yeah, that could work. That way I won't accidentally bump into myself." There is another one, they explain. They've identified another. Just in case this one doesn't work. There's another they couldn't find me in. They don't know if the me in that one has died or relocated to another continent or something, but I'm not near her in any event, so there will be no weird conflict if I go there. But they tell me that if I happen to run into myself in another timeline that I should be honest and let myself know what's going down and assure my other self that I'm not an imposter or evil twin out to do anyone any harm. They tell me to pretend that I'm a completely different person and that it's just a strange coincidence that I just happen to look incredibly like that other me there. And then they go about their business setting up what needs to be set up. "Good luck," they say in their clinical, scientific, matter—of—fact way. "Give us a call. Let us know how things work out," they point to the radio they gave me.

There is a technician who stays in the back, in the shadows. He hangs his head and shakes it from side to side every so often. Finally I approach him and introduce myself. He tells me his name is Hinrich, and he proceeds to try to convince me not to go ahead with this endeavor. He has a sad look about him—far—away eyes, furrowed brow, sunken cheeks, as if he has been living with the same uncertain burden hanging over his head for years and years. He tells me that he too has tried to follow his love from one life to the next, only to be rejected each time. "Your reward for living this life, for enduring, will be great in heaven," he whispers, "Just let it be, man," he looks down and shakes his head, "Your destiny is here, in this life, this world, this timeline. I know you're looking for a happy ending, but this is the way it is supposed to be," and he continues on and on with all that. "So how do you do it? How do you go on?" I ask. "I just keep reminding myself that today is just practice for tomorrow," he exhales heavily, stares off, then directs his attention to my face. "I appreciate what you're saying, trying to lessen the blow just in case things don't go well, but I'm willing to try every last thing here, so there's no need to lay all your past baggage down on me, man. People are always layin' down their insecurities and worst fears onto me—as if I'm to blame, as if their failings are my fault. There's no need for that here . . ." Desmond steps up to us, "There a problem here?" Hinrich looks over to him, "He's just anxious, that's all." I look over to Desmond, then back to Hinrich, "Hey, at least I'm tryin' here. . . I want to know that I have attempted every last thing I could before I call it a day and resign myself to the idea that it just isn't meant to be. . . At least I'm tryin'. I just can't heed your advice. I have to try. If I don't, I know I'll spend the rest of my life wondering what might have been if only I had tried. Perhaps my feelings are ruined beyond repair. But maybe in another lifetime our relationship will not be damaged, and I can live out my life with everything I've ever wanted. I can live out my life the way I feel it is supposed to go."

They position me in the center of the large white room and tell me to wait, my bag dangling at my side. "Will it hurt?" "Oh, no. Not at all. You won't feel much—some tingling and a flash of dizziness as the electromagnetic pulse ripples through you," and with that the technicians pull down goggles over their eyes and walk away. "Hey, how come they get to wear goggles?" I shrug, but no one answers. "Hey? Hey? Don't I get goggles?" "Naw," they call back as they walk, "You'll be fine. When the swirl of static appears, just walk into the center of it," they point casually as they disappear behind a door and into their control room beyond. "I'd like some goggles here. Can I get some protective goggles over here? Please? Hey, come on guys, if you all need them, then maybe it'd be a good idea to pass some on to me, you know, just in case. Hey, come on here . . ." I call out, but no one is around.

I hear a whirl of large electric generators start up in the next room. The floor vibrates as if the giant generators are gaining momentum, straining to produce a lot of energy. Maybe it's just not meant to be. Maybe it's just time ripping us apart—the fabric of space stretching us away from one another. I still have to try though, even if this is my only hope, my last resort, my final chance. I have to try to get her back. If not in this life, then in another. It's as if I've lost myself, and in finding her again, maybe, just maybe, I can reconstitute myself again. Maybe I can regain myself, re—becoming who I feel I'm supposed to be.

The air about me crackles and snaps. Sparks appear, spots and flashes. A whirl of static slowly forms in front of me, like the static from a television screen, only swirling in a ring. I step to it, the static engulfing me—all tingly and shocking the hair on my arms until the static gains momentum to form a ball of pulsating light around me. The light grows brighter and more intense, the current building into a blinding fury of silver and white. The swirling fury hits me with a shocking electrical warmth that zips through my body. I can not see. I have to try. I just have to try. I repeat over and over. I have to try. I have to try. I love her.

There is a rushing hiss in my ears, growing louder and louder until all is bright and I can not see or hear. All that is left is a high—pitched ring until the blinding flash of light subsides to flickers and strings and spots and my eyes adjust and I find myself standing in the park. It must be about noon. The sky is blue. There is a chill in the air. I am in the park, down by the river. I look around. Everything looks the same, except the church on the corner is painted a slightly creamy yellow instead of the white that it is in my parallel world. A large house on another corner that has always been dark green is now a dark red.

All is calm and quiet and peaceful and serene. I can't wait to re—meet everybody I know. I can't wait to see what they're up to in this place in time. I take a deep breath and start walking. Well, I guess I might as well try to find her.

the run

I wake to a slight pitter—patter. It is a faint scurrying from down the hall. The tapping grows to a mini—roar. I snap up in bed and turn to the hall just in time to catch a long stream of gray weaving by—a herd of tiny elephants thundering past my door. There must be 300 of them in all, kicking up little puffs and clouds of dirt and dust. The dry misty tufts waft into my room, partially obscuring the last of the tiny elephants as they pass. The elephants are the size of small dogs. They're just faintly illuminated by the light we keep on in the kitchen down the hall. And then there is nothing, just that weak pitter—patter, now fading down the hall. I exhale as I haven't drawn in a breath since they woke me a moment ago. I sigh and lay back down and roll over. It must be around 3 a.m. on Tuesday again, I shake my head. It figures. They always wake me about this time of month.

the new kid

I'm sitting in the library, waiting for study hall to start. It's the first day of school, so I don't know who's going to be in this session. I look around, hoping one of my pals shows up, hoping that Thalia girl I like happens in.

I've settled into a table in the far corner, away from everyone else, when suddenly a new kid walks up to me. I've never seen him before, but he looks like a real goof. He's kind of timid looking. "Mind if I join ya," he sings. "Sure do," I sing back, but he settles in across the table from me anyway. I thought that was a pretty gutsy move, but just the same, I sit there thinking: why do I always get stuck breaking in the new ones? Must be something in my face, a hidden friendliness that lurks below the surface that I'm not conscious of or something. I'll have to do something about that.

He slings his bag up to the table. I remain there slouching in my chair and staring at him with dull, bored eyes like: what gives you the right? The thing is, it doesn't look like anyone I know is going to show up. I'm concerned about this. I might actually have to get some work done here. And just as I look down at my books, the new guy goes, "Wanna play tabletop football?" So I slowly look up from my textbooks and give him a good, long staring, and then my boredom gets the better of me and I shrug and sigh, "Sure. I guess," eyeing him wearily as he smiles and reaches into his knapsack. I figure he's going to pull out one of those flat, paper triangle shaped football deals that kids use to push around on desks and tabletops with their fingers as a mock football.

But he starts setting up these little plastic people, lining them up like chess pieces. But they are not chess pieces. They are colorful little figures decked out in football gear. He is removing them from the side pocket of his knapsack. He has a whole pile of them. He begins separating them. "These can be yours," he explains without looking up to me. Soon there are two even piles, most of them standing up, but some piled together. One group has blue uniforms with red sleeves and red helmets with a wide blue stripe. The other team has yellow and white uniforms with purple trim. I lean in as the figures intrigue me. They are so cool looking, the detailing so exquisite. "That team is yours," he nods to the yellow ones, "That pile there," without looking up to me. "Wow," I gasp slowly, "These guys are really cool." "Yeah, I know," he agrees as he continues standing his little men on their feet. "My dad got them for me," he swallows, "On one of his business trips . . ." "Where?" I ask. "I don't know. He visits the Orient a lot," the new kid sniffs. "Now set your guys up, like this," he stands his figures up. I lean forward and begin to stand my guys up on end. "How do we play?" I ask. "We don't," he nods. "They play themselves. Watch."

They feel like plastic, like little scale figures for model train layouts. These models are about half an inch high, just little mites. "Here," he says, pulling a little counter from his book bag. "We keep score with this," he waves it. It's the size of a pocket calculator, with two plastic wheels on either side that you rotate to adjust the score which shows in little windows in the middle. He raises it to his chin, then blows a whistle in the middle of it. The whistle is very slight, but yet sort of like a football whistle that a ref would blow to start a game. Suddenly the tiny models leap into action. They jump up and begin running around, right before my very eyes. I haven't even finished righting them yet, and wham, there they go, off they run to the center of the table. The ones still lying on their sides spring to life. They run onto the field and form a kick—off line by lining up in a long, straight string. "Oh my," I exhale in disbelief, my eyes wide with wonder. "Yeah," the new kid nods. "Pretty cool, eh? They always do that. . . Don't worry, they know what to do." And sure enough there is a kick—off, my team kicking away to his.

A little ball sails up in a perfect arc. His team receives it deep in their territory and quickly performs a double reverse, the little guys cutting and scrambling and running great, wide, sweeping arcs in a dizzying swirl of colors and motion. I am shocked and speechless at the terrific spectacle. My mouth opens, but nothing comes out. Only stunned silence of disbelief. The double reverse hand—offs work, fooling my guys completely. One of his dudes scampers about twenty yards down the sideline. It looks like he might break it and go all the way, but then one of my little buggers catches him, arcing around to cut him off at an angle, trapping him, forcing him out of bounds.

The figures regroup, assembling in the center of the table in respective huddles. The huddles break and they line up for a play. The quarterback looks up to the new kid and the new kid mouths something to him and the quarterback turns his head to address my defensive line assembled before him. He puts his head down and calls out some whispered numbers and the ball is hiked and the players burst into motion again, the quarterback scooting and scrambling in an arc to the sideline, one of my guys is chasing, reaching out and tripping him up. He has a man wide open on the other side of the field, but the quarterback stumbles and loses his grip on the little ball. The ball finally slips from his grasp and tumbles, spinning and bouncing on the table. The quarterback stumbles and finally slides into the ground. A guy from my team who is trailing him scoops up the ball as it bounces in the air, circles around and advances the ball up to about the other team's twenty yard line before getting caught in the clog of players in the center of the field and eventually tackled by several of them.

"Man," I utter in a mighty exhale, my face aglow, my eyes as wide as dinner plates. "I—I can't believe this. This is an incredible game. How—how can they do this?" "I don't know," the new kid shrugs. "They just can." "They're—they're incredible." "Yeah. Yeah they are. I know," the new kid examines his team, mouthing instructions, leaning close into the tabletop. He looks up to me, "Just whisper. Don't worry, they can hear you. Their hearing is excellent," then dropping his head back down to the players.

One from my team walks off the field and stands in front of me, looking up. "What's he doing?" I ask. "Play," the new kid says. "He needs a play. Call a play." I look across the table to the new kid, then down to the player. "Long bomb," I mouth and the little bugger nods in acknowledgement, then turns and hikes back to the huddle.

Just then the teacher comes over, appearing from behind a tall bookshelf that has us isolated to a degree from the others. "All right guys," she instructs, "put it away. No games in here." I look up to her. Oh no, I think. "Get out those books," she continues. "I know it's the first day, but I'm sure you've got something to do." "Aw," the new kid groans. The teacher glares at us, then walks away. I look down and notice the players are frozen like miniature plastic figures.

"Dang," the new kid hangs his head and reaches his arm around and begins scooping his colorful football players together. "Hey," I lean in and whisper. "No. Don't. Let's keep playing, man." But he just shakes his head. "I don't want them taken away. That happened at my last school with my tiny basketball teams. . . Got myself in all kinds of trouble," he shakes his head. "Besides, we can play later on, after school." "Yeah," I nod in agreement. "That might be nice." "Yeah," he lowers his head, "Maybe you could come over. I got bigger ones at home," he shrugs, "And other junk my dad's given me." "Yeah, maybe. Maybe," I whisper, but I am suddenly unsure about this. This seems so odd and freaky. And not the good, surprising kind of odd. How do I know these aren't real people, somehow shrunken down in a zombie curse or something. Maybe this kid's parents are really voodoo people or something. Maybe some plane went down and some backwoods tribe happened upon them. Who knows. I'd like to play with these cool football players again, but maybe on neutral ground and not just at his house. "Maybe we could meet up here after school. The library's open till six. Or the cafeteria." I say as I reach into my knapsack and pull out a book. "Yeah, o.k.," the kid nods as he puts the last of his stiff little plastic people back into his book bag. "Right here, after school."

The kid looks harmless—pale, meek, kind of timid, but still, you never know. As I think of this, I began getting more wary of the whole thing. Maybe he is harmless. But maybe not. Heck, I'd play football with the guy, but there is no way I'm going over to his house alone. Who knows what's going on over there. Then he pulls out a book and says something that really startles me. He says, "So, let's hear about this Thalia girl. . ." The funny thing of it is, I never even mentioned her to him.

I glance up from my book and look him over every now and then for the rest of the study hall. If he could really read my mind, or somehow knew everything that's going on, then maybe he could read hers, or one of her friends. Maybe he could find out if she really likes me or not. I keep thinking about this until I realize that I'm staring at him in stunned silence for what seems like forever. I start to get mad that he knows my innermost feelings, my most private confessions, things I haven't told anyone yet. I feel, I don't know, not that he has invaded my soul, but more that he has somehow violated my trust by saying out loud what I am unwilling to admit, like he has passed on a secret that he shouldn't have or something. So curiosity and anger finally get the better of me and I blurt out: "How'd you do that?" in a stern whisper. "Do what?" he whispers back without looking up from his book. "Just read my mind like that. How'd you do that?" I lean in. He looks up at me. "I have this medicine," he swallows, "This vial of elixir my dad got. It's a special potion. About a half an hour after you drink it, you can hear what people are thinking. If you tune in and really concentrate—really really hard, you can actually hear what people are thinking. Really. No lie, man. You can hear a person's thoughts for about a half an hour. I just did it to you so I could tell if you were friendly or not. I mean, I'm new here and I don't want to get in with a mean or negative crowd. So how would I know? I mean, it's weird being the new kid. You wouldn't believe it. But I tell ya—I think I can help you out. All I have to do is take the stuff while she's around. That should do it. Say at lunch or after school. And then you come walking by and I'll be standing by her and I'll tune into her and see what type of reaction she gets when you say hello as you pass on by. That could do it, huh? Maybe?" he shrugs. "Yeah, maybe. I mean, I guess we could try that, but what's the catch? I mean whadaya want from me for it?" I ask. "Hey, I just need a football fan who knows what he's doing and who can keep his mouth shut about my game. I mean, I like play-ing, so I figure I owe you a little something in return so you don't rat on me, that's all," he shrugs. "You look like the type who knows when to keep quiet about this or that. Besides, you know about my game, and I know you like that girl. So we each have something on the other, which makes us even as far as I'm concerned," he leans and whispers. "Yeah, OK, fair enough. . . For now, I suppose. Where'd your dad score that stuff anyway?" I ask. "My dad's got tons of stuff like that. Gets 'em from his travels to remote villages deep in the jungles on the scattered islands of the Pacific. He's like a researcher guy, goes to old mountain villages in Western Europe, spends time in the wooded valleys of South America, the deep, smoky hollows of Appalachia, the backwater swamps of the Mississippi delta. He goes all over the place. Sometimes he's away for weeks at a time. But he brings me back stuff. Stuff he thinks will help me out in life. You know, he's the protective type. I tell him to let go, that he should want me to make friends and get out there, but you know, we move around so much it's hard to get to know people sometimes. Everybody's got their little protective crowd all developed and all that so it's hard to break into a new group sometimes. One time he brought me back a ten legged cat the size of a couch. I mean, you could ride it and everything. Anyway, he . . ." The new kid went on and on and we got to talking and I thought, you know, he's been relatively honest with me, and that's a good sign, so I guess I'm glad he decided to pick me to sit down next do. And I also couldn't help but keep wondering if that Thalia girl likes me or not. I mean, wouldn't that be something if she actually likes me?

people have been drifting away lately

People have been drifting away lately. Just out of the blue, here and there someone will lift off the ground and float off, slowly turning away into the sky. Just like that. I haven't seen it for my-self, I only heard of it, and I guess at the time I just dismissed it as a rumor or someone else's problem or something. I guess I was busy with my own thing—too busy painting my garage—scraping off the old and putting on the new, too bogged down with the dishes and laundry to really think much about it.

If it is true, maybe the floating away is just a symptom of all that—a byproduct of all that indifference, detachment, busyness, people hurrying through life, not stopping to con-template or appreciate. I know I get to feeling that way some-times—the days moving faster and faster and faster and things drift away from me. So maybe that was it—just some odd col-lective feeling, some vague notion in the air shared by all.

I sort of forgot about the matter, until one day I'm walk-ing down the way and I came to the corner drugstore. I stop to wait at the corner for the light to change and the traffic to clear so I can continue on across the street. There are some other people standing at the intersection and waiting there too. Some of them are waiting for the bus. Suddenly one of them sort of curls up. He is an older gentleman, all dressed up in an old suit. He seems to flatten out and his body sort of squares up. Right before me. He says, "Oh my," as this happens. It starts slowly, as if all the air is being sucked right out of him. And a bit of wind catches him and he sort of lifts off the ground and just hangs there in the air before us for a moment, then a gust of wind takes him higher—like twenty feet in the air. And he slowly spins there in the sky, almost like a leaf or a kite. It's like a dream, but like watching someone else's dream from a distance. I can't believe what's happening. It's all so fast we can't process it. We're all stunned, standing there frozen as the older guy just hovers there, the breeze sort of bobbing him slightly up and down, his now thin body just rippling and fluttering. Suddenly, I snap out of my trance and step into the street and try reaching and jumping to pull him back to normalcy. He is slipping away from us, away from humanity. We are losing him.

Another person jumps into the street and then another, joining me in trying to lower him down, to bring him back. Quickly we form a human ladder, me jumping on someone and another person being boosted up on top of me. But it is all too late, suddenly the older man in the natty old suit in the sky is just sucked away from us, his now flat body curling by the force of a mighty gust and then yanked from us, just whisked away, becoming but a dot slowly zigzagging out of sight and away from our lives.

We are stunned beyond words. I stammer a few gasps, but that's all. I am out of breath, horrified beyond rational thought. Someone calls the police and they show up, but it's all too late. The police report that this has been happening all over lately. We'll go and look for him, they say. We ask if they ever come back, if they ever land, if they ever return, if they are ever found? No, they say. So far no one has ever gotten snagged up in a tree or caught on a roof or anything like that. They just disappear, drifting off to nowhere.

This begins happening more and more. You'll see people in the sky, all flattened out, slowly spinning. You'll see someone scattering down the street, flat as can be, caught in the wind like an old newspaper. You'll see someone blow right by you. You try to catch them, reach and fumble, grab hold, hang on, but they'll just slip right by, off to who—knows—where.

No one can figure out what's going on or why. It's as if this is some strange new affliction. At first the authorities deny it's even happening at all. The phenomenon is dismissed as a rumor, a fairy tale, folklore passed down from our older brothers and sisters or from our cousins visiting from out of town, or an isolated incident at best. But gradually the evidence begins to grow, showing more and more people are drifting away from us, and it feels like there's nothing we can do about it. But even if the authorities officially deny it, at least we know it's been going on because we've seen it first hand. Many of us have seen it too many times by now and are about to give up hope of not having everything sucked right away from us or blown away to mix into the heavens above.

Some people live in fear, never stepping outside. Others take the attitude that if it happens then it happens. Me, I am one of those. By this time I have seen too many bad things, but refuse to be beaten down by it all. I figure it's meant to be, that some higher authority is behind it all and knows what it's doing and we will all be clued in as to the reasons soon enough. I figure it's all just a big puzzle, and that I'm merely a piece of it, maybe too small to see the big picture of it all just yet.

How can we stop all this? All this drifting away? That's about all I think about. I'm not worried so much for myself— I'm not married and have no kids, and plus I've gotten my affairs in order, just in case, as have a lot of other people, I assume.

And then I hear a rumor on the bus—that if you make funny noises it'll all subside. It will all go away. It seems one time someone was turning into one of those flattened—out leaf people things, the air being pulled right out of them and they were deflating and squaring up and they began to gulp and gasp and wheeze and trying to talk and scream and cry for assistance until only some funny, strained, strangled, gibberish squeezes out of their thin, flat body. The funny gibberish noises seem to relax the muscles and the contractions or seizure or spasm or whatever is happening. The relaxation of the lung deflation seems to slow the event long enough for people to get a grip on things, to have others grab them and hold them in place for a moment, force more air into them, calm them and talk some sense into them. And that seems to do it—just by making some funny noises, some unique squelches and sputters of sound and nonsense. Well that and just relaxing in general. But it is the sounds. The funny sounds. The general, all around: "eemmmbuugga neeeerrrrr wiiiiingggiiiinnnnddddeeee burumba douba linka scoooobbbaaa aggaahhh aggaahhh boogala—boogala," and all that nonsense. That seems to do it. Just releasing and celebrating the nonsense seems to do it.

But then I came across some others who happen to want to experience the blowing away, the drifting off, the getting carried away with it all, the riding on the waves and currents of fate. They are tired of the weight of their daily burdens and dream of casting off all the weight and gravity and want to blow freely and just drift without worrying about where they are going or how they are going to get there or where they've been and how long they need to get to the next thing. They want to escape this age of uncertainty. They feel this is all a very natural thing and a blessing for anyone who can see the bigger picture in what you are really meant to experience— different things, unique things.

Some people are into it. They're curious as to what is next and where the drifting will lead them. I try to argue with one of them at a party. I'm sure that we're meant to be together and that's what's important—helping one another grow and changing ourselves with the influences of others. But this one fellow wants to let go of it all. He says, "Let's take to the wind. Let's let go. Let's get lost." This does make some sense to a degree, but then, later on, I find he's really into free jazz and free association and all that magical thinking and talking and all that kind of thing, so I figure he's been on that whole vibe, that whole trip from the very beginning anyway, so he probably isn't one who has recently had any realization or inner discovery of any profound manner that would also help influence me in any way. Meanwhile, I'm on the side of staying on the ground, staying the course, trying to keep things together, trying to keep people from drifting away from me. I consider this a noble stand.

So we'll see what happens here. We'll see if any more people adopt the nonsense, the babble, the gibberish, the silliness. We'll see if they remember the magic of the silly gibberish, or if more people drift off. We'll see if any of them finds their way back to us. Maybe their experiences away will help them fill out into more complete views of things. I don't know what a perspective from the sky could provide, but gradually I must admit, the more I think about it, the more interesting it sounds. And I wonder if I will join them some day. I wonder: will I be willing to let go, or will I try too hard to hang on?

I found them in the weeds

big head

My wife looks over to me. Startled, she gestures her knife in my direction, "Honey, your head is growing," she squeals in surprise.

"What?" I say, lowering my fork.

"Look! Just look at yourself!" she gasps, cupping a hand over her mouth.

"Yeah, Dad, your head's bigger," my daughter leans inquisitively. "Does it hurt?"

"What? I . . I don't know," I gently place my silverware down onto my plate and slowly raise my hands to my face, touching my head—the top and sides and back. "Really?" I feel around. "I can't feel anything."

"Yep, that melon a yers is a swellin.' No doubt about it," my daughter studies me, her eyes narrow. She continues chewing.

"Do you feel all right?" my wife looks concerned.

"I think so," I respond, still touching my head, trying to gauge its size.

"Maybe we should leave," she whispers.

"Our food just got here," I shrug, nodding down to my plate.

"Yeah, Mom, I'm starved," my daughter swallows, her eyes not leaving my head.

"But your cranium," she furrows her brow.

"It's really getting bigger," my daughter squeals.

"It is honey. Oh my, it's really growing. Swelling," my wife frowns.

"It's gross, Dad," my daughter continues staring at me, then she looks over to her mother. "Let's get outta here." Then she looks back to me. "Before someone I know sees."

I continue patting my gourd. I want to stay at the restaurant. My wife and I are worried about our daughter. We're concerned about her eating habits. We suspect she hasn't been eating. Or sleeping enough. Or maybe she's sleeping too much. We don't know. We just suspect something. We don't know if this is a phase that she'll grow out of or something deeper. They say if your kids aren't eating, it may be a problem with their parents that is manifesting itself within the children. Maybe she senses something in our marriage, something missing, something wrong in our relationship. Maybe she is being affected negatively by something, some outside influence. Me and my wife keep graphs, and scales, and we chart everything we can think of, her movements, her company, her habits, we take turns following her around, hire a detective, things like that.

"Oh," I say, feeling around. "Oh my, this could be bigger," I stand up. "I better get to a mirror, check this thing out." I turn and walk briskly through the crowded restaurant, holding my head, trying to squeeze it back down. I move swiftly. Luckily no one notices. I quick-step down the hall to the bathroom, holding my head, pushing it in my palms, rushing to a mirror, any mirror. I bull my way into the men's room and stagger up to the sinks and look up.

They were right.

My head is bigger.

Quite a bit bigger.

Maybe if you didn't know me you wouldn't really notice right off, but this thing is becoming quite a melon. It looks all puffy and inflated. It is definitely bigger than most heads, getting out of proportion with my shoulders and the rest of my body—getting out of proportion with society. This is unacceptable. This surely won't do. To be different. So different. So cruelly, cruelly different.

Is it something I ate? Something in the potatoes maybe? Radon? Is it radon gases leaching in through the floor slab of the basement, its invisible stink poisoning my genes against myself?

Why me? I begin gasping. This couldn't be happening, not to me. I just made "Associate" at the firm. Finally, after years of sucking up, I had a title, a coveted little title.

I have to stay calm. Calm for myself. Calm for my family. I'm sure it's nothing, just a touch of the flu or something, just a reaction to something in the food. "Oh no," I utter under my breath, leaning in close to the mirror. "No. No. No," I rub my head with both hands. "Not me. Not here. Not now." I spin and dash out. "I've got a big meeting tomorrow."

I tell the matron to get my family, tell them to meet me out front. I run to the car.

On the way home I have to hold my noggin out the window. By this time it simply won't fit inside comfortably while I drive.

"Oh, gross, Dad. Groatie groatie groatie," my girl shrieks, looking away. "It's ballooning, Dad. It's ballooning."

Once in the garage, I run straight to our bedroom. The largest mirror in the house is in our bedroom above my wife's bureau. I huff out of breath, crouching to fit my face in the mirror. "Oh, man, it's bigger. It's bigger," I whisper. "What am I gonna do?" My head is enormous by this time—as big as a large t.v.—monstrously distorted mouth, gigantic ears, big googilly eyes, all flopping wearily on my shoulders, bogging me down.

"What should we do?" I turn to my wife as she runs for the door.

She stops and clutches the jambs with both hands to steady herself, then she catches a look at me. She just stands there trembling and shaking her head. Then she brings her hands up to cover her mouth again. Her knees weaken.

My daughter catches up to us. "Oh, my God, Daddy," she stomps her foot. "Come on Daddy, get outside. Get outside. Before it's too late," she waves.

I try to move, but my head is just so gosh darn big and heavy now. It totters monstrously on my now puny shoulders—teetering me this way and then rolling back again that way as I stagger to balance under its weight—staggering to the door, stepping forward and back, side to side, trying to even out and distribute the load, desperate to balance the crushing weight on my shoulders. "Oooohhh," I steady myself, watching my head growing in the mirror. I simply can not look away—a giant, comical pompadour forming, my knees buckling.

My wife screams as my head begins to crack the plaster of the ceiling. Stunned, she staggers back a step or two.

"Ow," I complain, my now stubby arms reaching up to try and rub my fantastic head. "That hurts." But I only reach the sides of my puffy, inflating cheeks.

"Come 'ere, Daddy," my daughter holds out her arms from the hall. "We've gotta get you out of here," she huffs out of breath from the panic. "Let's get you outside," she bends at the knees and claps her hands as if calling an unintelligent puppy. She drops to her knees and slaps the floor with her palms.

I lower myself to crawl out, but my neck gives out, flopping like a limp noodle, slamming my head into the wall next to the door. The momentum of my big, goofy head thrusts me forward, my head bounces off the wall and flops to slam on the floor. "Ow." I push with all my might, bulldozing my big head to the door.

"Come on Daddy, come on," my daughter slaps the floor in encouragement. "You can make it!"

But by the time I get there it is simply too late. I am out of breath and can't squeeze through. All I can see is floor. Just carpet. "Get a doctor," I wheeze, "Get a doctor," I pant, flailing my arms as if trying to swim my way out the door.

My daughter turns and runs. It don't think she's running for the phone. It feels more like she's escaping in terror, abandoning me here like this. My wife just stands there hopelessly. Out of the corner of my eyes I can just make out the bottom of her quivering legs.

They must've been out in the driveway waiting for the ambulance. Surely they heard my screams as my head began working its way through the siding, creaking and bulging like a baby bird cracking to split through its egg shell.

gilbert, the sexy robot

Part 1

My friend Boone calls me up. He claims to have built himself a robot. He says he's going to use it to help him attract women. This sounds like an intriguing idea as Booney is not having any sort of luck in finding a nice girl to hang out with. He invites me over to see it, to show it off for me. He is so excited. I can't tell if he's happy because he accomplished such a feat as building an operable android, or if he's just excited about the potential for pulling in some gals. So I head on over and sure enough, in the middle of his workroom down in his basement stands a gleaming metal robot.

Boone is really into robotics and tinkering with electronics and that sort of stuff. He even has a little workshop-type lab in his basement. It's pretty impressive. So it only stands to reason that he'd try to build a large person to keep him company and help him out around the place with chores and such—dishes and laundry and vacuuming and dusting and mowing and clearing out the gutters and all that. Having someone to help with these things will free up a lot of Boone's time to do other fun things like reading or playing around in his lab. He envisions a day where we all have our own personal robots, liberating us from having to waste so much of our time changing light bulbs and shopping for shoelaces and such. He envisions a day where we will have more room for rest and recreation, more space to tackle social issues and medical problems, more time to help elevate society to the next level. Maybe one day we will all have more time.

So I show up and he's down there dressing his robot and applying the synthetic skin—covering the head with a face and the long, thin metallic arms with skin that look like long gloves or sleeves or something. He flicks a switch in the back of its head, and it begins to move on its own. I'm very surprised. The robot is impressive. Astonishingly, startlingly so. It is remarkably life-like, appealing physically, and has a gentle nature about it. And I must admit there is something about it that makes me want to hang around him and get to know him and trust him and even seek his approval. Maybe it is his height, his stature, his solidity, his gentlemanly demeanor and good looks. I don't know, I'm not really sure, but I must admit I'm very impressed with the technology, the intensity of will, the rigor; however I'm a little concerned about the motives behind the project. Boone tells me that nothing else has been working for him girl-wise lately. He says he doesn't want to resort to buying a puppy to use to lure women, or lift weights and such as his body is just fine the way it is, and that he just doesn't have the time anyway. I mean who really does after all?

"This thing is supposed to get you dates?" I inquire skeptically, yet as supportive as I can given the circumstances. "He's supposed to approach women and ask for their numbers for you? Or he's just going to meet the girls first, so you can hang out with their friends later, after he introduces you?"

"Yeah, man," Boone stands and steps back to admire his creation. "This baby 'ill attract a ton a chicks with the unbelievable, massive, raging superstardom of his rockin' rollitude. And maybe, just maybe, I'll be able to skim up some of the leftovers," he folds his arms. "Yeah, this dog is it, man," he beams with pride.

"Well, why don't you just approach the girls first to begin with?"

"Naw, girls don't like guys like me, man," he shakes his head. "But they like guys like Gilbert here—tall, strong, good looking. A real dreamboat. . . Yeah."

"Boone, you're a scoundrel. Why would you want to hang out with anyone who wouldn't want to hang out with you in the first place? Why not find someone who's going to like you right off the bat? Someone who likes you for you?"

"Too hard to find. Takes too much time," he points to the robot. "Gilbert here will draw 'em in so I won't have to," he shakes his head. "I got stuff ta do, man."

"Sounds too complicated."

"No. Not at all. I got it all planned out. You see I pretend that I'm Gilbert's roommate, which I kind of am anyway. So it's not like some terrible lie or anything. I mean, what else am I supposed to do? It's only a minor deception. A diversion. Like a slight-of-hand trick a magician may employ, that's all. I mean, I need all the help I can get in this area. It's what I want. It's what I need help with. Who else is gonna lend a hand? Huh? You? Hell no. No one wants to help people anymore, they only say they wanna help. But they never actually ever get around to it. Just saying they want to help is enough to convince and fool themselves that they're helping you out. So here is Gilbert, the sexy robot, programmed to help me out. Programmed to meet the demands that I can not—that of providing me with time. The most valuable of all commodities. He will help me around the house, thus providing me with more time to con-centrate on other endeavors. He will go out and meet people for me, so that I don't have too. He will sort through them and bring the nice ones back here, freeing me up to do other less time-consuming things. You see? He is providing time-saving services. It's what I want. It's what I need. I mean, everyone wants or needs something, right? So who are you, or anyone else for that matter, to judge me? I mean, what do you want? What do you need?"

"Me? Emm. I don't want or need anything," I consider, "I

guess I'm happy with what I got."

"Nothing? There isn't anything out there for you?"

"I guess I'm just happy to be alive. I guess I just want to live. To just be alive. That's probably good enough for me. I mean, I've got plenty of interesting books and movies and music tapes. Tapes by the box full. Slot cars and kites and all that. So I can't see the need for anything else without cluttering up my life, gumming up the works and clouding up the clear view that I possess at this time."

"Well, I respect and admire that, but me, me, I want more."

"Aren't you afraid of using technology to fill a void that should be handled from within. Not through artificial contrivances?"

"Your books and tapes are artificial. Right?"

"I guess."

"So you see, this is just my version of that. My variation on what you already have in your life to help make you feel complete and whole and what helps you have fun."

"I suppose," is all I can offer.

"Me, I need time, man—sweet, precious time," he gestures to his creation as if the robot itself represented huge blocks of hours to inhabit and long, stringy stretches of time to fill. "Gilbert here represents freedom, you see. Freedom, sweet freedom."

Part 2

I don't hear from Boone for days. He tells me about the test run. Evidently he took Gilbert out on the town. I guess he performed admirably. Things went so well that Booney sent his robot out solo the next night. "Perhaps it was a little too soon," he mutters.

"Why's that? Did he break down or something?"

"No. No. Nothing like that. I think he's running fine. Maybe too well."

"What do you mean?"

"Well, I think you better come over here," is basically all he says.

So I rush over.

And sure enough, there he is, lying on the floor amid a terrible mess. Apparently there was some sort of power struggle and Gilbert, the sexy robot, ended up taking off on him. Gilbert wanted to assert his independence as a separate, free-thinking being and just upped and left. Booney tried to stop him, at first physically; but obviously Gilbert being an incredible robot, just overpowered him with one swoop of his metallic arm. Then Boone tried to reason with him, employing psychology, sentiment, and nostalgia by putting on Gilbert's favorite song—Grand Funk Railroad's "Shinin' on." Apparently Gilbert was half way up the basement steps when the song kicked in. He stopped and stood there for a moment, then looked back, down on Booney, and just said, "I've got that recorded in my memory bank," and then continued up the steps and out the front door. And just like that he was gone. Boone yelled after him: "You go ahead. Just go ahead! I don't want you anymore anyway! You won't last three hours out there on your own without me! So go ahead. We'll see what happens. We'll just see," Boone spit bitterly from the floor. He was very upset.

I guess Gilbert grew to want pretty much what I want— just to be free. To be alive. Maybe he's a little like me in that he really doesn't need much either. It sure seems like he didn't need or want Boone anymore. He is synthetic after all. I mean, the guy could stand out in the rain all day and not get sick if he wanted to. He's made of some special alloy. He wouldn't even rust. He just wanted to be on his own, to be alive, to exist, to go where he wanted when he wanted, to experience things—to just be.

So me and Boone call some of our friends and go out and look for Gilbert. Boone figures that he built him and housed him and thus he feels that he owns him. He feels that Gilbert belongs to him. Boone even wears his working overalls just in case ol' Gil wouldn't recognize him in his regular street clothes. Marcus and Mathias and Cinchy show up, and we all set out to search the bars and dance clubs in town. Boone figures that's where he'll end up as he is programmed to meet people and to clean. And since the day is for cleaning and the night is for meeting people, he'll most likely be out and about by this time as it is getting late. So we split up. But we don't find him on our first night out.

Since we have to work at our jobs in the day, we can only look for him at night. This search takes us to some interesting night spots—pig wrestling spots, drive-in theatres showing old westerns, community theatre, you name it. But we don't see him for several nights, until Cinchy ends up spotting him at a diner down by the river. He calls each of us on our cell phones and we converge. When I get there, Gilbert is at a booth with several luscious babes around him. Gilbert is wining and dining them, his winning smiling glowing like a newborn in the night.

We're hiding and peeking from around a corner, from out of a hallway that leads to a delivery entrance. We figure Gilbert has earned some loot by doing odd jobs around town or working as a maid in a hotel or something, as cleaning and yard work are his specialties.

Boone has brought some rope and we agree to jump Gilbert and hog tie him outside in the parking lot when he tries to leave. We figure Gilbert is mightier than any of us, but together we can maybe contain him and shut him down, flip the switch.

We wait and wait until finally they all get up to leave. We follow them out and sure enough, it has clouded up considerably and starts to sprinkle. The next thing you know there is this horrific crack of thunder, and before we can even make our move, Gilbert, being made of metal, is hit by lightning. He is leading the women to a car when zap, he is struck by a mighty blow from above. A flash lights up the parking lot. Gilbert's head shoots straight up into the air. The women are knocked down, and when they finally shake off the momentary effects of the blow, they look up to see this body just standing there, smoldering and without a head. Finally gravity does its thing and sends Gilbert's heavy metal robot head plummeting back to the surface after about a one hundred and fifty foot shot into the air. His head hits the pavement with a great ear splitting crack! And startled, the women run off in all directions, just as I would've done under the circumstances had I not known that Gilbert was only an android—as charming, good looking, confident, and well mannered as a robot can be, given today's available technologies.

We walk over and Booney picks up the head. It is damaged beyond repair, still warm and smoking from the blast. The women eventually make their way back too, recovering from the initial shock after running a few blocks. I mean, they have to return to get their cars anyway. Dejected, Booney explains the situation to the girls. They seem upset at first, but a little flattered that someone would be so shy as to resort to such extreme measures and expend such energy in trying just to meet them. One of them ends up giving him her phone number, which is all that Booney really wanted in the first place.

Boone gives up on robots. After Gilbert, his heart just isn't in it anymore. We encourage him to continue, but he just can't seem to recover from the loss of Gilbert. Gradually he begins to concentrate his mechanical interests into go-cart building. We meet up with him a few weeks later at one of the competitive go-cart races. We speculate he has disassembled Gilbert, or maybe uses him as a very large and elaborate doorstop or something. You know, just to keep him around and all, as a reminder of a special milestone or accomplishment, or just for the company. I ask him about it, but Boone just shakes his head and looks away and mutters something about Gilbert being no more. No more. I figure that he must have taken him apart then. Maybe the thought of ol' Gil just standing there so cold and unalive is just too much for Boone to bear. That's understandable, I suppose, Boone being his creator and all.

He seems just as proud of his new creation—his gleaming, sporty go-cart, standing before it, nodding his head and looking down, "Yep, this baby 'ill impress the ladies all right," he smirks with hope. Funny thing though, we figure Boone's going to pilot his own go-cart, but sure enough some other big guy walks up and takes the seat. The driver of Boone's souped-up ride looks sort of like Gilbert. "Oh no," Boone assures us. "That's just Mike, a guy I know." This seems suspicious though, as none of us has ever met, or even heard of Mike until this very moment.

thank you

I hear a noise. It wakes me. Sounds like something dropped. And then a slight rolling sound, like a marble rolling across the wood floor of my bedroom. I tumble out of bed and flick on the light. And there on the floor before me is a large round marble. At least it looks like a big marble. I bend down, pick it up, raise it to my face and examine it. It seems like a large pearl—all creamy swirls and hard. It's the size of a nickel. Then another slowly rolls out from the corner of my room. My birthday plant sits in that corner. I look over and notice a leaf uncurling itself at the base of the long, flowing plant.

My grandmother gave me the large plant for my birthday last week. I thought it was an odd present to give to a kid, but then what do I know. The plant sits on a wiry metal stand about two and a half feet off the floor, with dark green vines and heavy leaves cascading down to the floor from a yellow ceramic planter.

The second little marble rolls slowly and then stops in the middle of the room. It must have rolled out from the leaf, down a vine and onto the floor. It stops right before me, right about where the other was resting. Now I remember. Grandma took me aside at my party and whispered to me that it was a very very special plant and that I should take extra good care of it.

I reach for the second pearl, pluck it off the floor, raise it to my eyes and study it as well. It is the same as the first one—only a little bigger—the size of a quarter, a little heavier, and with a tinge more cream.

Then I look over to the vines and leaves flowing from the pot in the corner.

"Thank you," I hold up the pearl and nod to the plant.

the bug

A big ruckus wakes me. I listen intently to gauge its origin. A rattling stirs from some unknown depths of the basement. I open my eyes and just lay here. What else can I do? The rattling bangs with a sharp conviction and certainty. It is not late at all. Just twilight, with the last of that orange fading on the horizon. The lavender and pink rises to meet the navy blue that's coming down to close up the rest of the day, that navy blue closing the day up like a trunk until it's time to open it all up again in the morning.

And as the peach and pink swirl, the distant banging returns. Maybe it's a burglar breaking in through one of our basement windows? Perhaps he's down there, lurking about, hoping with a dingy gray glee to run amuck and do no good, hoping to mess the place up but good. Well, not on my watch, pal. I slide out of bed and slink down the dark gray hall with my trusty baseball bat, ready to bash a noggin.

I grip the bat tightly and sort of practice tapping an invisible noggin as I tiptoe through the muddy darkness to the basement stair. I hear the ruckus growing louder. I hear my pulse racing, my heart beginning to knock in crazy anticipation to knock a noggin about. I picture my various swings and strokes of the bat—a chop from above to the top of the gourd, a roundhouse wallop to the tummy, a diagonal slash to the shoulder or midsection or jaw. "Aim for the jaw," a tiny voice whispers from the fuzzy depths of the back of my mind. I slide through the kitchen, my breath held in hope, heart beating, calling, shouting, banging, and that ruckus splitting the serene twilight.

I flick the switch in the back hall to the stairs. The light screams a blinding white blast, and there is dad at the bottom of the steps. His back is to me and he's moving about oddly and shaking, as if being electrocuted, or as if attempting an odd teenage dance from his youth—novel, creative, twitching movements that I don't understand.

I lower the bat and he turns his head to look up at me with a foreboding glance, shaking in a forced, tight, controlled struggle. "Dad," I utter under my breath, and finally he turns to reveal a frantic death struggle. He has a large bug in a choke hold. The bug is his size, with a long, thin thorax and oodles of wiggling, long bug legs gripping him all over. "Are you dancing?" I ask in confusion.

"No. . . No son," he gasps as they struggle.

"Do . . . do you need some help?" I stammer helplessly, not knowing what to do.

"No. No," he huffs, "I think I got 'em," they sway back and forth. "I can take him. . . . I can take him," he grimaces, but it's as if he's only trying to convince himself.

"I can bash his noggin, pop," I chirp optimistically, tightening my grip on the twenty-eight ounce Louisville slugger. Every single ounce a death in waiting. Every single ounce ready to go, and me ready to leap down behind them.

"Now there's no call for that, son. No need at all," they twist around in a tight clutch—a great epic struggle playing out before me—my dad and a giant, ugly bug, gripping tightly, holding one another as if they almost need one another, as if they need the struggle to keep pushing themselves along, to keep moving themselves forward, to get them up in the morning. "He took my newspaper again," my father delivers an impressive haymaker to the breadbasket, and then a tremendous knee kick to the tummy, and with that the lanky thing curls up around his fist. For just a split second its many many legs seem to wiggle uncontrollably, and then it's as if the thing seizes up and freezes for an instant. Then it goes limp, flopping down to hang over my father's arms. "Open the door, son. Open the door," my dad lifts it and puts it over his shoulder to support it, as if lugging a great weight—like when he brings in the sleeping bags after camping. He adjusts the heft of the bug and swings it around and begins climbing the stair.

I gasp for breath as if I'm watching the entire breadth of history somehow unfolding itself before me. Frankly, I didn't think my pop had it in him. I beam with pride and shake my head in wonder and awe as he lugs the hairy, leggy thing up the steps.

"Stinkin' bugs get in through the cracks in the foundation. I tell ya, I caulk and caulk, but every year one of 'em seems ta manage to find a way in. They try an' make themselves at home down here. In the cool of the basement," he huffs and climbs, balancing the heft as he labors his way slowly up the steps, each careful step at a time. "I tell ya, every year," he shakes his head.

I turn and fumble for the door. I open it quickly and spin around as my father grows larger, him and the limp bug getting closer, my heart pounding like a giant drum. And I swear I see the legs twitch, as if the thing is coming out of it. "Dad," I whimper. And sure enough the legs begin moving. I jump out of the way and draw up the bat, ready to do some big time damage, ready to splatter an enormous bug.

My dad glances up. Suddenly one of his fists fires a blur from down low, cracking the bug between its large, wide, sickening eyes. "Whack!!!" It's head and legs go limp and flop back down again as my dad heaves it out the door as if tossing out an old rug. I watch from behind as the thing tumbles and rolls down the back steps. My dad slowly walks down to it, bends to reach for some of its legs, swings it around and begins dragging its limp body down the walk to the trash out in the back alley. "I call this one Artie. . . . Man, I tell ya," he sighs, "They never learn."

"You've seen this one before?" I gasp.

"Oh, sure. He knows the place pretty well," Dad nods, ". . . He slept in your bed one night when you were staying over at your friend Terry's place."

"Oh yuck."

"Yeah, they like to make themselves at home. You should've seen him there—snuggled up all warm and cozy like. Your mom actually took a picture of him. Said he looked cute. Before I yanked him outta there that is. . . That was one rude awakening alright. Caught him a good one with a frying pan. Pwwaaang! Right on the ol' noodle."

"Wow," I whisper as dad drags him out back.

"Yeah," he exhales, "that's why I always sleep with a can of bug spray clutched in my fist under the covers. Just in case. You never know when they're finally gonna get smart and start showin' up in numbers."

giant chicken menacing me from above

I've wasted my life. Mostly through being afraid. I don't even know what I'm afraid of anymore. (Fear of rejection? Fear of being alone? Fear of social embarrassment? Fear of the confinement of absolute conformity?) It all seems so contradictory.

I've finally figured some stuff out though, coming to some final, gravelly realizations by laying out my problems, sorting them into a fine grain of categories. The calculations indicate that all my missed opportunities were because of fear—me being too afraid to act, too afraid to make any decision at all, for decisions lead to consequences, action can lead to failure, and thus social embarrassment and a crippling lack of confidence or faith in even the most basic of everyday objects.

I figure I've been too passive, letting things pass me by, least I get caught up in them. I hide in plain sight by being a bystander in life, always off to the side, out of harm's way, hiding from it all. And what good did that ever do? Where did that ever get me?

I pray that the carnival spirit will visit me and set me free, but nothing ever comes. I try everything—poking fun at the inner existentialism of the lonely starkness of the modern design magazines, inciting brawls at rural pancake houses, faking flamboyant panic attacks at solemn basilicas, joining my friend, Chris, in egging on the apocalypse, hanging out at laundromats, studying the entirety of Gilligan's Island in depth—hoping to find the secret of life hidden amongst its many layers of meaning. I try many things to not hide, to not be so passive.

Really, I think I just want to live within my dreams, but obviously I can't enter them, revel in their comfort, fly through a cloudy warmth. And then I grow frustrated that I can not attain this ultimate comfort.

I've been thinking about this a lot, about all the missed opportunities adding up, about being afraid to act, unable or unwilling to move forward, about hiding in my own life, about hiding it all away, about creeping low in the shadows. I've been thinking of stepping from the safety of the shadows of doubt and indecision, into the enlightenment of action and response. But instead of drawing me out of the shadows, all that thought and consternation only seems to bring a giant chicken, fierce and mean.

I think the giant chicken is a manifestation of my fear. It may be an escaped science experiment, or just some plain ol' chicken that wandered off a ranch and became irradiated by some random leak or poisoned by environmental toxins, like in the old monster movies.

My encounters with the giant chicken progress as such – I'm slinking through the back alleys as always, when a great, nasty shadow comes over me, looming from beyond a building. My eyes shoot up and meet its dark, impenetrable, little BB dot eyes. There it is—a giant chicken.

As if by some mythic power, I cannot look away. It's as if the giant chicken has locked me in its view. I've never seen anything like this before. Suddenly it looks down on me with derision, obviously sickened by my cowardice.

It stares down at me. Then raises its head and long neck over the one story building between us. I'm in awe at the dark shape, now looming over my shoulder as a vague gray outline.

It startles me to see a towering thirty-foot-tall chicken in the middle of downtown like this. I cannot move. I just freeze for some reason, stunned that something like this could exist without people knowing about it. Maybe it escaped from some lab, maybe from the university several blocks away.

Gradually I come to my senses, but notice no one is running or screaming from it. For it is standing on the street-side of the building. Surely others must see it. The damn thing is just standing there, coolly looking me over, examining me as if in disgust or shame.

I stare back at it, more in confusion at first, to see such a banality out of scale like this is so strange. Then my confusion turns to wonder and awe, and then to fear as it reaches to peck at me. It lunges its long neck as if to pick at me (like most people seem to want to do these days. There is this need in the air—this urge to pick at me which encircles me, following me like a fog, as if people were disgusted at the notion of my very existence, that people were disgusted that I wasn't like them, a duplicate, a clone, and thus felt I had rejected the very essence of their being, their life-style, their beliefs, all that they were, and thus I was an enemy and must be destroyed at all costs, as trying to convert me would simply take too long).

The great, filthy bird reaches to peck, but can't stretch far enough over the parapet to actually reach me. Realizing this, it recoils and lifts its head to the fates in anger and frustration, letting out the most blood-curdling squawk you could ever think to imagine (an angry, giant chicken squawk of rage). I snap from the moment, jump and dash away, but again, am careful to listen for others—various screaming and panic. But I hear no one. It's as if everyone's inside for some reason, or as if I'm the only one who can see this giant chicken (now alleged, as I have not touched it, thus am somewhat skeptical of its existence myself. Perhaps I'm dreaming or hallucinating. Perhaps I'm having an episode).

I find myself scooting through the back alley shadows and

refuse, creeping low, darting from shadow to shadow, for I have become shadow matter, refuse matter, invisible. I scamper away, somehow knowing that the giant chicken is here for me and me alone—searching for me as if a manifestation of all my combined fear and failures—my failure to act, to get off my butt and do something, expecting everything to be done for me, expecting things to just happen.

I make my way free of the situation, but know deep in my bones that the giant chicken is still out there, looking, tracking me down, lurking, waiting in the shadows, in my shadows, always waiting . . .

After a few days, after my initial scare has receded, I sort of forget about the giant chicken that menaced me from above. I consider that maybe it's not after me specifically at all, maybe its just some random big chicken—lost out there, frustrated by this, or in a bad mood for some reason—just some ill-tempered big chicken.

It may not have been after me specifically, looking to punish me for being too cautious, too passive. I start to think, aw, naw, get over yourself, man, it could not have been after just little old me. Surely I'm not one of those who thinks that everything that happens on this planet is about themselves. Maybe it's just some sociological experiment, attempting to measure how various people will respond to random stimuli—in this instance, a very large, ill-tempered chicken. Maybe it had gotten free of some laboratory—some giant breeding program to get the most from livestock.

Gradually, I forget about my run-in with the great fowl and the entire scare, until a few days later when I'm in the supermarket parking lot. I'm loading my '67 midnight blue Plymouth Fury station wagon (with mag wheels) when I feel something behind me. Another great shadow moves over me. I stop for a moment, and know it's there.

Slowly I turn and there it is, looming above the single-story supermarket, a vague form coming into view as it steps around a corner, appearing from behind several four-story apartment buildings. It stops and stares right into me. And I know it wants me. I can just tell.

I turn and run, abandoning my car, the folding back door still unfolded, half the bags still in the shopping cart (a flash of thought blasts through my mind—a bright orange flash—maybe it's a good thing the giant chicken is after me. Maybe it will knock me out of my complacency, help me see things in a different way, as if my entire life I have been waiting to be told what to do, what to think).

I scamper through the parking lot, around the maze of cars, through the glaciation of shiny metal death boxes, between the metal coffins, looking back over my shoulder at the great bird stepping on top of the building, walking over it onto the parking lot with ease, then calling out a loud, menacing chicken cry.

"Aaaauuuugggggghhhhhh!!!!!!" I scream in absolute white-hot terror as I dash into the alleyways, flailing my noodley arms, huffing in panic, abandoning common sense and all that I previously knew to be true.

The giant chicken chases me through the back alleys, almost as if chasing me through the back alleys of my own mind. This all seems so unreasonable—that a super large bird would want to hunt me. Immediately I begin to lose faith in what I had believed to be true, in what anyone had ever told me, in simple, everyday objects. At that moment I realize that I simply can't trust anything anymore. In fact, I had been a fool to even consider trusting anything in the first place. Even simple objects become suspect—a brick, a two-by-four, a rock, an alarm clock, a mailbox. I am through with them all.

The great bird's shadow looms over me, covering me, but I dash around this corner and that, under this tree, around that garage, through a back yard, through a garden, the bird undulating its neck and stutter-stepping until we reach a narrow turn and I am able to make my escape. I hit a spot where several four story brick buildings are, and find a narrow passage between them. The bird can't get around the buildings, and can't squeeze in between them either. I run into that tunnel of alley, obscured in dark shadows, the bird looking around, sticking its head in the opening, trying to get in but realizing it cannot. I watch in relief over my shoulder as I huff and run frantically.

As I creep in the shadows, I wonder if that thing will be waiting for me everywhere. Were there more of them out looking for me? Could anyone else see them, or had I lost my grip on things? Had I lost perspective? Had I lost faith in the stability of everyday objects and routine? I hadn't had time to stop and ask anyone if they'd seen the great bird. Maybe it was only real to me?

Slowly, cautiously, I make my way through the shadows and alleys, back to the supermarket parking lot. It takes hours of crouching low and leaping from shadow to shadow. Periodically I see the great bird's dark shadow against a building, or just catch the top of it's dingy white feathers peeking over a building or distant tree line. But it seems I'm always a block or two away from it.

I stop at an entry point to the parking lot and look around, waiting to make sure. There's my car, waiting out in the open with the bags still in the cart, the back gate still folded down. I sit for a while, then make a dash for it, out into the open, the bright blue sky welcoming me, me spinning and running, looking around. I get to my car, throw the bags in, push the cart away, jump in and speed off.

I get lucky this time.

I get home and research chicken repellent, but can't find anything that will stop a beast weighing several tons.

I lay low for a few days, not going out at all, not even looking out the windows, or even going anywhere near them. I stick to the shadows of my insides. I'm reduced to crawling on the ground, but I don't mind. There's no way some chicken's going to get me. I ready a large poker, fashion it from some stray items in the garage—a long curtain rod and an old boat anchor. I figure maybe it's best to fight back. Maybe only then will it leave me alone.

After a few days I finally go out again. The coast looks clear. I ride my bike down to the parkway. I like the winding stream that passes through, the soft trees and greenery, the picturesque simplicity of the winding path. But sure enough, after about twenty minutes of riding, that damn bird peers around a large clump of trees and spots me.

I skid to slow. The mangy beast is about a hundred feet ahead. Our eyes meet yet again. I lean to turn, peddling like mad in the other direction.

I wonder if that thing has waited for me, crouching low, disguising itself behind bushes and tall trees, only to leap out at the sight of me (but again, maybe that's a good thing, maybe it could forever remind me not to be so passive, not to forever wait for things to come my way, that I should go out and take action on my own, not to be afraid of consequences, not to be afraid). But I find myself still afraid, and this fact begins to disgust me. So I whip behind a large set of bushes and wait. I hear it coming, lumbering between trees. I pull the long poker from my knapsack and wait.

When I feel it's time, I leap out, jabbing one end of the poker into the ground to steady it, lean to drive it into the soil, squint to see if I can recognize the angry chicken, to see if it's the same one that scared the wits out of me the other day, hoping it will see my resolve and stop and look me over, considering me as a man of courage and determination, and thus respect me and see that I am not worth its trouble.

Soon it comes lumbering around the corner, crouching low, head darting, trying to locate me. It spots me, squawks a terrifying screech, raising its head, strutting, then lowering itself to charge, head first.

I steady myself as it rushes forward, my legs going numb, my arms shaking, a voice in the back of my head screaming in fear, and yet another voice calmly realizing: 'Oh, so this is how I die.' Death by giant chicken. Death meted out by the great chicken of doom.

The chicken chugs down the walk, into the grass, its large feathers fluttering in the rushing torrent. I gulp and go numb, for it is a fearsome sight. I know I'm going to die, but I'd rather not die a coward. I'm tired of the fear, tired of the senseless waste, sickened by my own existence and what the fear has robbed me of—all the missed opportunities, all the lost time I could have applied to getting good at something.

The air seems to get sucked from the scene. Things go quiet. It's just me and the giant bird now, big as the canopies of the trees lining the little green clearing we now share. The ground thumps with its running. The bird hits the long pokey stick. The stick bends, then snaps, sending the chicken backwards. The great bird staggers, trying to regain its balance, its huge wings fluttering, creating a wind that blows dust, dirt, sticks, leaves, and stray blades of grass to swirl in the air. I cover myself, then instinctively realize I have a chance. I dive out of the way, roll to the tree line to disappear into the shade. Once in the darkness under the trees, I dive into the thick brush that borders the winding creek. I roll down the bank into the shallow water, come up and run across to the other side. The bird bursts through the trees and bushes, thrashing its great head and neck around, squawking an anguished call. I stop dead in my tracks, out in the sunshine, exposed in the open, halfway across the narrow stream. I turn to watch.

The bird locates me, slowly walking down to me. I run in the water, to the other bank, crawling into the bushes on the other side. I burst out the other side and dash under some trees. Luckily there is a street right there, with a line of cars parked at the curb. I roll in the grass, under a pickup truck and lay flat on the pavement, my chest heaving, panting hard.

The bird steps over the bushes, then ducks under the tall trees to stand in front of me, looking all around. I turn and crawl across the blacktop until I'm several cars away. I look back, over my shoulder. I see the bird crouching low, looking under the cars a few cars behind me. I turn ahead and begin crawling faster, my clothes becoming tattered and filthy.

I still can't tell if it's the same bird or not. Perhaps it doesn't matter as I become lost in the moment. A mighty crunch grows in the air. Striving to avoid notice, I turn to see the bird leaning into the truck I was under, nudging it over as it leans its shoulder and neck and all its weight into it. Once the truck is balancing on its side, the bird straightens, jerking its shoulders and neck back and forth the way chickens do, looking around for me, until it finally, slowly, turns and lurches its heavy way back to the creek. It looks all around as it ducks to fit itself under the mid-sized canopy of trees, then disappears beyond the bushes.

I hear it splash in the shallow creek and see the top of it as it steps over the bushes on the other side. Then it disappears from view as I lay on my stomach under a car, panting heavily, heaving in and out, watching from the shadows. And the weird thing is that right then and there, clothes shredded, covered in grime and scrapes, I realize that I shouldn't stick to the shadows, shouldn't hide it all away, lest the giant chicken return to peck my eyes out, crack open my skull with its powerful beak, nibble away my brains like so many undulating worms. I figure I should stick to the safety of the crowd. For how could it discern my presence from any other person out there?

I stick to the crowds for the next few days, one eye on the horizon, waiting for the shadow of the great bird to loom again. I wonder if and when the great bird will appear, how it will chase me, what I'll have to do to get away. I figure I should get in better shape. I take to lugging around a large fire extinguisher. I strap it to my back, just in case. Maybe I can use it to scare the bird away.

I think about what it all means, what's it all for? Why a giant bird? Why me? But I have no idea. Could be just about any reason. Could be the fear drew it to me. Too much fear pulled it in like a magnet. Could be something else, someone telling me something. Could be nothing at all, just random. No rhyme or reason. Or it could just be my imagination. Maybe a hallucination, a fever dream, some undefined illness slowly showing itself. But how can you know which for sure? How can you trust any of those options? And does it really matter? If a giant chicken is after you, does it really matter the reasons? Isn't it enough to just have to deal with the bird itself?

I survey some pals: "Ever see a big chicken roaming about?"

"At the state fair once, I guess. But when I was a kid."

"I mean a giant one, like thirty or forty feet tall."

"Ah, no. . . Never even heard of one. You're the only big chicken I know of."

Their answers are basically in that similar range. After I ask around, it seems like some of them are no longer my friends. I don't know, it just feels that way. I figure maybe one of them might have heard something, but after asking, some of my old friends seem to keep their distance. Maybe they just believe in different things. Or maybe they have their own giant chickens to deal with.

just before the cattle started disappearing

I had overheard my parents talking about it. I heard my dad mumbling to himself about it, just thinking out loud, just wondering—shaking his head, referring to some guy as a "scientist" over and over under his breath, just whispering to himself, every time he came back from the feed store. I remember when that guy moved in up the road—into the Dupen's old place. He didn't even come around and introduce himself, an' I never seen him in town—not even at church.

One time I went to town with Dad. Mr. Hickey at the feed store was scratching his head under his hat. He had all sorts of pens and a cigar sticking out from the top of his shirt pocket. The sheriff was there too with his little black book. It was open on the counter. The sheriff was a big man with a stubbly burr haircut. He was wondering about some stuff that guy down the road ordered. Some "hormones" they were. Mr. Hickey said this guy had been getting packages—big and heavy ones—from some lab down south. He said he used to get packages from all over. Just little ones at first. But lately he'd been getting the big ones in.

That night I was sitting on the edge of my bed, looking out the window, listening to the cool breeze in the trees and the baseball game fading on my radio. And that's when I saw it.

I wasn't really looking at anything, or really thinking anything, just sort of day dreaming, just sort of dozing as grandma called it.

It appeared out of nowhere, just sort of floated up to the window. I heard a big noise—a loud mechanical flapping, a buzzing hum, a droning rumble, like from a radio controlled airplane or an old metal fan. Then I saw its shadow outside the window—a creepy, ominous shape. It bumped up against the glass. It made a "Bbbzzzzzzt" sound, like a far-off saw. It floated up to the window and I froze flat as a road. It moved in closer, right up next to the glass, as if it were trying to look in, as if it were checking things out.

Its wings were making the loud buzzing—rattling up against the glass, trying to get my attention as it hovered.

It was the biggest bee I'd ever seen in my entire life. It was bigger than a large watermelon. I mean the thing was a giant. It just hung there, humming like the biggest barn fan. It must've come floating around the corner of the house, right to my room from out of the woods. I can't really remember it that clearly as it all happened so fast, like a strange dream. But I must've heard or sensed it coming because I turned to look out the window. And there it was, just hovering there, bobbing up and down in the air.

The air was dead silent, like it wasn't even there at all, like that gigantic bee had chased all the life out of the air. The thing of it is is that it's so heavily cool at night around here, but this was a different feeling—like a brittle stiffness, or an emptiness—like the air wasn't even there at all, as if that giant bee had sucked all the flavor right out of the air.

The thing just slowly made its way to the window, into my view and hovered there, buzzing away. It was the most awful, gut-turning noise. Then it moved even closer, as I stood there. It filled half the window. I tell you, I just froze. The blood rushed right out of me. And then I gradually turned all hot for some reason, my eyes bulging at that sickening beast—sweat tickling, prickling my skin. And that's when it happened. It sort of .. I swear, I swear, it sort of looked at me, as if it were staring at me. I can't really describe it—but it was as if it had been looking for me, looking for me as if it knew me.

the procedure

A mother wakes her son in the middle of a deep dark night. She leans over his bed. His stillness, his warmth rises off his unseen sleep. "Son," she whispers to the darkness, holding back a twisting forest of emotion. "Your sister hasn't been feeling well lately."

Her little boy is ascending from sleep, shaking off his stiff, rusty repose. "What time is it?" he squints at her in the darkness, then rolls over.

"It's late," his mother answers, her hush of voice quivering, sitting at the side of his bed, looking down on his dark figure.

"What? . . What?" the boy looks around. His arm flops. A cold wind blows outside, rattling his bedroom window.

"Your father had to take her . . . to the doctor," the mother gulps in a forced whisper, trying to get through his sleep without touching him. "He just sent word. There is a rider outside."

"Do you have to go too?" the boy slides up, sluggishly rolling his head on his bony shoulders.

"He sent word. . . I have . . . I have to tell you something," she swallows hard.

There is a dark silence.

The boy is trying to hold his head up. He senses the rider at the door, the big warm brown horse outside, its puffs of foggy breath against the window, its head shaking in the cold of the rough darkness.

"They're coming home," she whispers, "They're on their way."

"They're coming home?" the boy repeats, trying to stay awake.

"She's been very very sick. It got worse. Much worse. There was an accident. She didn't get better . ."

"She's coming home? They're on their way now?" the boy yawns.

". . . She didn't get better. They had to," the woman chokes. "I just had to tell you. . . She wasn't getting better. They had to perform . . . a procedure," the woman chokes again. "She wasn't getting any better," she shakes her head, looking down and then turning away from her son.

"I'm thirsty," he says through another lazy yawn. "They'll be home soon?"

"They're on their way now. We'll get you some water. But they'll . . . They'll be home soon," she reaches both of her arms and pulls him from the mountain of blankets, tugging him from night, tugging him from sleep, lifting him and swinging him out his bedroom door and into the hall and down to the living room.

The little boy is still wrapped in a blanket. As his mother swings him to the floor, he spins from the twist of cloth to stagger into the living room, lazily stepping to the direction of the kitchen. He steps into the living room and just then, through the big picture window, he sees them coming up the walk. They climb down from a carriage and begin walking. They appear as shadowy figures. His sister is walking ahead of his father. She is still in her pajamas, nervously clutching her stuffed pig in her hands, but she doesn't look like herself anymore. She is just movement in the oily darkness, just a gray outline, but as she emerges into view, her father's lantern flickering in the blackness, he notices it.

"Mommy," he utters, growing weak in the knees—sinking and leaning—for his sister now has the head of a goat—all gnarled hair, protruding snout, and little horns—a look of shame in her tiny, beady, black marble eyes.

"She's . . . she's been sick," his mother swallows hard, "There was an accident. A terrible accident," she gasps, "There was nothing . . . this was all we could . . . she didn't get better."

The boy is ushered off to bed, but does not sleep. He feels terrible seasons of heavy winds inside him, as if holding him back against any hope of long, restive sleeps for the remainder of his life. He feels empty and drained, powerless against the countless wild whipping winds. He feels tingly and numb, and gulps for air as if all the air in his room has been sucked into those swirling torrents roaring inside, leaving only old, dry air—ruined air. He feels betrayed by life, as if a promise had been made a long time ago that these things would never happen, and here something like this was now suddenly allowed, without preparation or warning, as if his sister were sacrificed so others might live out normal lives free from the reaches of such things.

The next day he tries to make the best of it. He tries not to stare, yet also to not look away. He tries to make things seem as they always were, as if to set things straight.

After breakfast they sit around playing cards, or trying to play cards. His sister just sits there on the floor, kind of slumped against the couch. She doesn't move much at all and when she does her movements are stiff and tight. Her shoulders sort of fold in with a shameful posture about her. She doesn't look at him. She just gazes a blank, empty stare off to the side, or down at the floor. Maybe she is trying to add up and assemble what has happened, maybe constructing in her mind what the rest of her life will be, what she can manage to gather from a broken, incomplete break. The boy is hoping she is still groggy from the procedure, or from being up so horribly late. Maybe she is still burdened by the weight of her affliction.

He hopes she will emerge from this temporary fog and return to her normal pep, eventually resume her running around the house, or out cutting paths in the fields.

The boy sits there, handling the cards nervously in his lap, looking down at them as if this were all that life has left him with and he is trying to figure out what to do with them. Finally, he looks over to her and studies her and her little matted goat head. He leans in a little to see if everything is all right. He studies her eyes. They are like dim, black marbles, with a dull, hazy glaze—a dull, glazed look about her, an ashamed look.

He leans in and tries to see into one of those little black garble eyes, but there is nothing behind them. There is nothing there at all. He only finds his dim little reflection floating as if lost in there, as if some tiny little someone is trapped way deep down inside there, trapped and struggling to get out.

little giants (behind the barn)

Bullies chased me home again. Some bigger, older guys. Real morons with nothing better to do. I gave them the slip under the bridge at Anderson's Creek. I scurried through the drainage pipe and lost them in the tall weeds and sand of the sand bar.

I cut through the cornfield, still running, not knowing whether they were right behind me or not. I turned and headed for the pasture, out of the corn and into the long grass and over the hill. I hit a patch of short grass up on the little hill and ran under some trees. I glanced back, but no one was there. As I looked back, I tripped over a tree root and landed on my face in the dirt, slamming into the hard, dry ground with a slap of flesh.

I gasped and hacked and spit sand from my mouth. I rolled over and sat up and wiped the dirt from my face, trying to catch my breath. As I brushed sand from my arms and legs, I looked back to the little valley sprawling out below me, undulating hills and mounds of trees, fields everywhere, with winding sandy roads cutting quilt-like swaths, tiny creeks meandering through like rips and tears and fringe. I had never seen this area like this before, from this vantage point, sparkling in the sun, long, thin clouds filling the sky, great lumpy, dusty trees spotting the rolling landscape, stone fences winding this way and that into the hazy distance, and the wind in my face.

I was glad to be alone now, sitting in a peace and quiet of

breeze, relieved to be away from everyone at school, all the meanness, all the futile competition and social climbing.

I rested under the shadows of several old, tilting trees. The trees leaned and curved into one another. The gentle breeze calmed me and whirled in the branches and leaves. I looked around. There was this odd little barn behind me. It was small, like an overgrown shed. It had imploded, folding down to the ground. I had never seen this barn before, even though I was born and raised in the valley.

I turned to examine the crumpled mess of dry boards. I thought about crawling into it, turning it into a fort, hiding stuff in it—candy and fireworks and stuff. Unfortunately there didn't seem to be much head room, so maybe a little hideaway was out of the question. The wood was all rotted and gray and the roof slumped in the middle. It looked almost like a playhouse. As I studied it, I gained a better sense of its scale in relation to its distance from me. Distance can be deceiving, you know. I reached my arm out to it and squinted. Why it was only the size of a couch, way too small to be a playbarn for there was no head room.

Just then I heard a faint humming. I looked down to see if a bug had buzzed between my legs, but all I could see, in the sand and tufts of grass, was a tiny tractor puttering along. It looked like a toy, like a very very small model.

My eyes grew as big as golf balls. I leaned in, and sure enough there was a little man on it bobbing in his seat as he drove. As I leaned, my shadow covered him and he looked up at me. My jaw dropped as he smiled and waved. I couldn't believe it. Here was a tractor the size of my thumb humming past my feet.

"Come back tomorrow," he cupped a hand up to his mouth and yelled up to me, "I'll show you some stuff. We'd all like to meet you," his tiny voice peeped. He spoke with an unfamiliar twanging accent. He spoke as if he knew who I was, as if he was expecting me.

"Yeah, alright," I whispered. "I will," I nodded in awe, without even blinking.

He looked ahead as he bobbed, but then gazed back up at me, over his shoulder and raised both of his arms. "Look, no hands," he chuckled as he puttered along.

"That's pretty good," I nodded. "Who are you? Where you from? 'Round here?"

"Oh, we've always been here," he chirped in his tiny voice. "For a long time," he gestured his arm to extend a wave beyond the valley. "One day, a long long time ago, we ran out of room, just used it all up. We were out of space, and then, suddenly, it was the most unusual thing, slowly we all started shrinking, the world around us growing and growing. An' I mean everything. Until we stayed this size. And now, here we are," he spread out his arms and looked around, "It's been this way ever since. . . And now we are all around, with plenty of room. Room for everyone and everything."

"My gosh, you're . . you're so small," I gushed in disbelief, crawling on the ground to follow his little tractor as it bounced along.

"Oh, that's funny," the tiny farmer chuckled. "You're a funny one, you are. Ha ha. Where I come from I'm quite large. Perhaps a giant even. A giant, if you will. Ha ha."

"That's amazing," I whispered to myself.

"Say, we're gonna test some of our weapons out tomorrow," he squeaked, "Maybe you wanna show up? Huh? We have many enemies we need to protect ourselves against—spiders and bugs and such. In that regard we have a lot in common."

"Ants," I nodded.

"Actually, for some reason the ants have always left us alone. I guess we aren't to their liking. Anyway we manage to co-exist . . . to get by that is. Maybe you can lure those bullies up here, maybe show them a thing or two!" he giggled, "You'll wanna see this. Ha! Trust me!" And with that he puttered off, into the long grass and weeds, disappearing into its shadows and deep textures.

now we can buy a monkey

red ball jet
(drop me off on planet earth)

Aliens appear in my bedroom. They wake me by shining some kind of weird blue light in my eyes. Jerks.

I shake my head and sit up. At first I think, oh great, aliens—that's the last thing I need right now. Yeah, aliens, that figures. Yeah, that's about right. But then my curiosity gets the better of me, and I wonder what kind of battery their strange blue light thingy takes. Probably a couple of double A's.

It's incredibly late at night. Two of them are looming at the foot of my bed. One of them reaches to me as my eyes adjust to the gray, foggy night. I'm a little scared at first. A little intimidated. I study their outlines—kind of a ghostly gray. They possess a rather ghoulish pallor. I sort of feel sorry for them—being all washed out and gray like that and all. They really should get out more—get some sun.

One of them raises his hand and begins to speak to me telepathically, putting pictures in my mind. He asks me what I want. I tell him I'm tired, that I just want to be left alone. I tell them to buzz-off, that I want to get some sleep. He says, no, we mean if you could have anything you want, you know, like a wish—if you could have anything right now, at this exact moment, what would you want? What would you like to do? Where would you like to go? What would you like to see?

I must admit I'm rather taken aback by this unusual proposal. I think for a moment. What do I most want or need at this time? Right now? . . . Actually, I was rather frustrated. It had been a really boring weekend. There was absolutely nothing going on. Nothing at all. Now I don't mind layin' low every now and then, just chillin' out and all, but this was the beginning of summer, I should be out there after all, out there wandering around, meeting people, hanging out, immersing myself in the soft, dark, velvety night. I tried to call a bunch of people, but no one was around. . . . Just then, in reading my thoughts, the alien asks me if I want to go out. This is a strange thing, to have some big gray dude talkin' to me in my head. His voice is all long and fuzzy, like out of a metal tube or a long concrete tunnel.

I think for a moment and shrug. Sure, I say, I guess I'd like ta go out. Maybe to a nice party that has lots of nice girls and some great tunes. Maybe to a cool club—some little dive. Heck, I wanted to go out all weekend and here it is Sunday night—and it's too late to do anything, surely everything is closed up by now. What a waste. Then the gray chap asks me how this makes me feel. I say I feel kind of bad about it—it being summer and all. I mean, I don't want to waste my summer or anything. I mean, I should be out there—out there doin' stuff, rockin' out or something, I shrug, and here I am, stuck here like always. I explain to him that it feels like I'm missin' out on stuff, that I'm wasting the summer, wastin' my life. Wasting it. Missing out on things. Squandering chances. Chances slipping right past me. Squandering my life away. What a rip-off. What a shame. Like here I had this great weekend, and what do I do with it? Huh? Nothing. Shoot some hoops and read some science fiction and watch some baseball and stuff. Read some baseball stuff and some Vonnegut and all. Yeah, sure, I cranked some tunes and all, but still, I just wasn't up for just hangin' low. I mean, it wasn't necessarily my fault. I mean, I tried and everything but nothing was goin' down. No one was around at all. But still.

I think the guy can tell I'm being sincere, that I'm bummed out, regretful, ashamed— feeling pretty bad about things, because he turns slowly and looks over to the other guy. Then he slowly turns back to me. O.k., he says in my head, we'll take you out. We want to learn more about your feelings, your inner-workings. I tell him that would be fine, but nothing's open, nothing's going on, it's too late. It's just too late. He looks back over to the other gray guy again and then back to me and tells me it's never too late, that there's always plenty of time. Then he asks me where I'd like to go if I could go anywhere, if I could actually be anywhere right now.

I smile a kind of crooked, disbelieving grin out of the side of my mouth, as if to say "get out of town." But the dude assures me we can go absolutely anywhere, that we can do absolutely anything. And I am instantly filled with a strange sort of faith, a warmth of trust rushes over me. For some reason I believe them. I mean, they're aliens after all, surely they could just whisk me off to anywhere. I mean, it just figures.

So I think about it for a second. If I could be anywhere, where would I want to be? If I could experience absolutely anything, what would I like to do? What would I like to re-do?

I remember always being disappointed that I missed the UFO concert back in '82. I think I was sick or something, I can't remember. That woulda been a great show—Saxon, UFO, and Rainbow—what a line-up, I shake my head. Then there was another really great show, The Only Ones and The Flamin' Groovies back in '78. That wasn't hard rock, though, that was more new wave, modish, power-pop stuff. Yeah, that woulda been something, to see those guys in a small club. A small new wave club. I shake my head. Man, that woulda been something.

I'm looking down, shaking my head and thinking about all the great shows I've missed, all the concerts I coulda seen, all the great times I coulda had, when suddenly I'm standing in a well lit bar. Suddenly we're back in 1978. They've whisked me back in time. Just like that. I'm dressed in some weirdo 1978 clothes. They tell me this is to blend in, so no one catches on. The two aliens are here too. Huh, imagine that. And sure enough, they're disguised as regular folk now too. So I look around, and here we're standing by the bar. We get to drinking and talking and I ask them their names and where they're from, how they like it here and all that. And they tell me their names, but the bar is noisy and their voices in my head are kind of foggy and distant, so it ends up sounding something like "Red Bull Jeff" or "Rag Bulges" or something like that. Maybe it was "Redball Jet," or maybe that's where they're from. Aw, in the excitement and noise of the bar, well, you know how it is. So I just start calling the taller one (the leader guy) "Gray Guy" and the other one "Junior." They just refer to me as "The Subject," which seems fair enough I guess, I mean since we're giving each other nicknames, it only makes sense they'd wanna pick one out for me and all.

Anyway, the bands crank up and it's totally awesome. Unbelievable! I feel like the luckiest guy in the entire world, like I've died and gone to heaven, man. We party. We rock. We hit the sunken dance floor and start rocking out like demons. The big guy just kind of stands there and shimmies—I think he's just playing it cool and all, checkin' out the scene. But Junior's really giving it his all—swaying and dipping and swinging around and hopping up and down like some goof who hasn't been out in way way way too long. And I tell ya, man, he really looks like he needs it too. I knew a night on the town would really do me some good right about now, but I never in my wildest dreams could've ever come up with this scene. It was simply, like, the best time of my life, man.

The bands rip into their best stuff—"Shake-some-action,"

"Another-girl-another-planet," the works. Celebratory, ebullient songs of summer, exuberance, and anti-conformity that also happen to rock enormously. The uninhibited music's beautiful freedom rings in the night forever. Then the bands end and the house lights go up. One o'clock and closing time. Time to go. So I look around, hoping we can meet some girls and hit an after bar party or something. But then I come to. Flash-of-light and I'm in my room, lying back in my bed like nothing has happened at all. Zip. Just like that.

I lay back and think, huh, that's odd, they didn't even say goodbye. But it's late and I'm, you know, kind of tired after the extensive and gigantic rocking-out I've partaken in. So I roll over and think about the night. It's all so vivid in my mind—bright and soft and moist and squishy. The bands, the clothes, the little club, the music, so clear and radiant, the atmosphere, the spiky hairdos, the bright colors, the oranges, the browns, the dankness, the girls. What a night. A dream come true. It totally made my summer. And what a comforting thought that is, that I wouldn't have to worry about totally wasting a summer on doing nothing fun at all. What a death that would be.

So I'm laying here, smilin', grinnin' from ear to ear when I hear something in my bathroom. My sister and I share a bathroom upstairs, like on the Brady Bunch—it's in between our rooms and we each have a locking door into that bathroom. But the weird thing—she moved away to college so it's all mine now. I mean, she hasn't come back home yet. She hasn't returned. Her school's not over for the year yet. That's really odd. She wasn't here earlier. I mean, what's she doing back home right now? This late?

I look over and the light's on. "Hey, who's there?" I call, thinking maybe it's the aliens still, Big Gray and Ol' Junior checkin' out the medicine cabinet or something.

"Jack?" my sister, Becky, replies. She steps from the bathroom, the light shining in as she stands in the doorway.

"Yeah," I answer sarcastically, like who'd she think would

be sleeping in my bed at, like, a million o'clock in the morning. And here I am wondering what she's doing home.

"Jack, how'd you get there?" she asks.

"I've been out, but now I'm back," I grumble and roll over, away from the light. "I, ah, snuck in. So I wouldn't wake anyone." I have to lie. I mean, what if someone noticed I'd been away. I figure the aliens flashed me back in bed somehow—slipped me in the window, or floated me in on that slick beam of blue light of theirs. Yeah, I gotta get me one a those blue light things. I bet it can do all sorts a stuff, better than a Swiss Army pocket knife.

"Jack," she calls again.

So I answer, "Ah, yeah," even more sarcastically. And then, suddenly I appear in the doorway, standing next to my sister.

The me in the bathroom says, "Yeah, whadda ya want?" He's brushing his teeth.

And Becky looks at him and then back over to me, and asks, "Who's that in your bed?"

So I say, "It's me, ding-dong. I'm in my bed." I sit up and the light from the bathroom catches me, illuminating my face. The eye's of the me in the doorway get bigger and bigger. He stops his brushing. His toothbrush drops to the floor. Becky clutches the doorjamb to steady herself.

Despite our shock and discomfort, we get to conversing and I explain what went down, and we figure the aliens must've drank too much or got lost or something and accidentally sent me back to the wrong time. We must've stayed out too late. Dang, I always seem to do that, don't I? It's one of my worst tendencies. They sent me forward in time, but returned me three years too early. And the next thing I know it's like a billion o'clock in the morning and here I am, lying in bed next to myself, all tired and all, stuck back in time. Out of time. Stranded. Marooned. Trying to figure out what to do now.

Part 2

Naturally the younger me wants to talk. He's asking me all these questions. And I start getting a little upset. I mean, I'm tired and a little frustrated that they'd leave me back here, and I'm tryin' ta get some sleep over here. I had a lousy weekend, then I got rousted by some mysterious aliens for reasons I don't even really know why, I'm out all night, then here I get stuck back in time. And now I'm really tired. Now how'm I supposed to deal with all that? Huh? It's a little much to deal with right now, you know.

So eventually me and the younger me start fighting. "Get out of my bed," he grunts, pulling the covers more over to his side.

"No," I say, "you get outta my bed—go sleep on the couch," I grab and tug back.

"No way, man. You go sleep on the couch. This is my bed."

"No it isn't, I'm older, I've slept in it longer, it's my bed. Now scooch over."

"Oh go feel yourself."

"Yeah, like you haven't done enough of that already."

"Oh shut up."

"No, you shut up."

So, we're going back and forth like this for a while. Then my sister opens the bathroom door, "Give it a rest already," she calls, telling us to shut it off. The little me hops out of bed and tries yanking the covers off. I pull back. He starts pointing, jabbing a finger in the darkness, poking me in my ribs. My sister stands with her hands on her hips, insisting, siding with him. "Yeah, imposter," she accuses. "Why don't you just get outta our house, this isn't your house anyway, you don't even belong here, why don't we just call the cops and let them decide."

And I'm all like, "Whoa whoa whoa, o.k., hold on now, how 'bout I just try the couch then, hey. Or we could all just cool out an' get us some sleep already 'cause it ain't like there ain't nothin' we can do about it right now anyway, so let's all just cool down here and figure things out. Let's all just get us some sleep. I mean, I realize this is all highly irregular and all, 'cause it's like this crap don't happen to me often neither, so cut me some slack here, I mean, I am still your brother no matter how old I am. I mean, gee whiz, what'm I supposed ta do about it? Huh? I mean, I'm some kinda genius here? Some kinda astrophysicist or quantum mechanics guy?"

"It's the government," Becky shakes her finger in the air.

"It's not the government," I sigh, exasperated, "It's the stinkin' aliens already. I got 'em all liquored up. We were just havin' too much fun."

"Yeah, the aliens," the younger me throws up his hands, "They're worse than the jivin' hippies already. What we gotta do is get us some guns, an' if they come back, whoa boy, we show 'em a thing 'er two about earthling hospitality by puttin' a couple a extra belly buttons into 'em, ya dig," the little me gets all excited.

I just roll my eyes. "Oh, that's right," I groan, "you must be in your 'gun' phase. How 'bout we all just get some rest instead. We can assign blame and finger point tomorrow. There's always plenty a time for that, ya know."

"Don't boss us," Becky snaps.

"Hey, I'm the oldest here, remember," I explain, pulling up the covers and rolling over.

"You're not the oldest here," Becky squeals.

"Yeah I am. Older an' wiser," I nod.

"No, no, no you're not," she insists, "I'm the oldest."

"Not anymore you're not—technically I'm, like, three years older. Remember, I'm from the future. So I say, lights out," and with that I close my eyes.

There's a faint glow through the bathroom from Becky's room. The glow flashes out as she stomps back to her room. The younger me stands there in the darkness for a while. I hear him breathing, thinking. Then he/I finally makes his/my way over to my/our bed.

Finally he climbs into bed and re-joins me. "Scootch over," he grumbles and I inch over a little. "It's my bed," he whispers.

"It's my bed too," I respond. "Only I've been sleeping in it longer than you."

"Yeah, but I've been here longer. You don't even really belong here. You're just a guest, remember?" After a while of lying in the darkness, he asks me if I think they'll ever come back for me.

"I don't know," I respond. "I suppose they will. Probably. They seemed to have a pretty good time. You shoulda seen 'em. They were really gettin' into it. I'm sure they'll be back. I mean why wouldn't they? They seemed like decent enough folk and all. I mean, you know, other than gettin' snagged back in time, hung up, caught here like this, other than that, all things considered, they were actually pleasant enough fellows. Very polite and well mannered, although a little on the mysterious-secretive side. . . Yeah, I'm sure they'll figure it all out," I yawn.

"Either way, you'll have to lay low," my younger self whispers.

"Yeah, probably," I answer. "Say, it's been a long night an' I'm kinda hungry. Think you could run down and get me a pop-tart 'r somethin'?"

"Get it yerself," is his answer.

So I say, "Hey, I gotta lay low, least someone sees me and freaks out and all."

The night spreads deeper and thicker, and as I lie there I start realizing how I was actually back in time. Huh, imagine that. I mean, think about it—what if I could go back and change things, redo things, undo things, correct mistakes in my life, regrets—you know, lemons into lemonade, silver lining and all that. So I sez to myself, I sez, "You know, the World

Series this year is kind of a shocker. You might wanna get in on the action. Heck, you could put a bunch of money down on the Super Bowl, World Series, the works. All the cake you can. Then hide the winnings in a safety deposit box. Hide the safety deposit box key in our Heavy Metal movie sound track album so I'll know where to find it when I get back to my time. That way we'll have a lot of money to spend in the future. I'll write all the winners down. You just hide the list in the album sleeve and refer to it from time to time. There's a bunch of bookies in bars around the college. They're easy to find if you've got money. Just ask around. Save up every penny you have and place bets with a bunch of them. We'll clean up. Really. This is good. This 'll work. I'm sure it will," I grin with pride at my perfection.

The younger me sighs, "Yeah, that's not a bad idea. What else? Tell me more. What girls like me?"

"Oh, yeah, that's a good one," I agree. "In about six months you're gonna meet this tall girl named Liz. . . ."

"Yeah?" he jumps.

"Yeah," I nod.

"Is she cool?" he squeaks.

"No," I shake my head. "Stay away from her at all costs. Trust me. Just stay away. Resist all her come-ons. Believe me, it won't be worth the trouble. Now, there's this other girl, Jill. You won't think she's interested in you at all. In fact she'll go out of her way to ignore you and be kinda nasty to you, but she's just being shy, kinda freaked about her strong feelings for you, that's all. She's not very experienced in matters of the heart. When you think of it, it's kinda sweet in a way. . ."

"No it isn't," I interrupt myself, "I'd go with the nice girl. Why waste your time with the one who doesn't even talk to ya?"

"Just trust me," I assure him. "She's interested in you. And the other one isn't nice, she just acts nice sometimes."

"Yeah? For sure? You're not just jivin' me here are ya? Pullin' some big, elaborate, nasty, time-traveling-big-brother trick on me here?"

"Naw. Don't worry about it. Here's what I think you're gonna need ta do ta pull it off. Now this might not work, but it'd be totally worth it if it does. First you gotta . . ."
Suddenly a flash of white light blankets the room, zzzaaappp, fffffffoooooooommmmm, and then in the corner there stands ol' Gray Guy and Lil' Junior. They tell me they're very sorry, and that they've been looking for me everywhere, that they'd lost me back in time and it just took forever and that they were afraid of gettin' in trouble and on and on and all that, and I'm all like, "Hey Big Guy, it's good ta see ya." And I look over to Junior and I'm all like, "Hey Tiny, how's it hangin'? That was some night there, back in '78, huh? The two of us just shakin' it all out back there, just livin' it all out, hangin' out together, just hangin' lose. Dang, Slick, we gotta do that again sometime, and I mean real soon—and that's for real, daddy-o." You see, I'm not mad at them, I figure they'd figure it all out and be back for me eventually—it was just a matter of time. I always sort of suspected this was maybe all a part of their experiment anyway. So here they're standin' there, trying to look all sorry like, thinkin' I'd be sore at them, and here I'm layin' here all relieved to see 'em. Ain't that just the way though? I mean, wouldn't that just figure?

So I list up a bunch of sports scores for me to bet on, then I turn to the guys and apply a little guilt. You know, the whole, gee guys, how could you leave me back here. Gosh, I thought we were friends and all, I mean come on here, and finally convince 'em to take me back again.

I consider going back and checking out a good basketball game. Maybe catch a Clippers game from when they had Lloyd "All World" Free or Bill Walton or something. When they had those cool blue uniforms.

Or maybe I should try an exotic, panoramic locale this time—a setting I'd never get to see—some place romantic, in-

103

triguing. Maybe head to Europe. Maybe hang out in Paris back in 1963. Catch some smoky basement jazz joint. Shoot around on a Vespa scooter. A little baby blue number. Scoot around with Audrey Hepburn or something. Hang out with an early 60s era Audrey Hepburn and wear those cool wrap around sunglasses. Yeah, Hepburn in Paris. Audrey Hepburn. That'd be fine. Really nice.

But instead we end up at a kickin' Sammy Hagar concert down in Texas, circa 1981. Yeah, an early 80s Sammy Hagar concert. But not just any Sammy Hagar concert. No, it has to be a Texas Sammy Hagar concert. And just like that—flash— we're right there in the middle of it all. And when Hagar rips into Montrose's "Space Station #5", I tell you I just lose it, man, just lose control of my faculties, just totally lose my mind. I tell ya, I start rockin' out like a mad man . . .

welcome home

You're staying over at a friend's cabin. It is a little log house deep in the woods. You all stay up really late, sitting by a campfire and telling secrets.

The night is terrifically black. Tall, dark trees loom all around. Rocks and scraggly grass encircle you in the foreground, as thick underbrush and more long grass rise to frame the distance. You are surrounded by a haze of golden light from the little fire that pulsates a peaceful orange glow.

A shadowy figure appears from the woods, parting the tall weeds. You reach for the closest person sitting next to you, and you grip his arm tightly. The tall stranger walks past the fire. You look up and he nods at the gathering and continues into the darkness. "A woodsman," someone whispers as the stranger disappears back into the shadows.

Later on, several more men emerge from the darkness and happen upon your gathering around the small crackling fire. Their feet shuffle on the hard ground. They each nod politely as they pass. They seem to be returning from somewhere. After they've re-entered the wilderness of night, someone else mumbles, "Prospectors. . . . Miners."

The fire goes down and the night sinks deeper into itself, and eventually you all retreat to the log cabin. You end up sleeping on the couch in the living room. Your friends share the bedrooms. You fall into a fuzzy, oily kind of sleep, but seem to sense heavy shadows moving about from time to time.

The next day you all swim and fish in the morning, make a trout lunch from your morning catch, and hunt and play in the bright, leafy woods in the afternoon. Later, you eat a supper of the rabbits that you caught hunting. Then you all enjoy a hike in the woods at night, through the grass and rocks of the meadow and under the cool canopy of forest. You walk along a stream and pass a pack of three prospectors. They are hunched over a corner of the narrow creek, under the umbrella of bright green trees. The clear water ripples under their large pans as they shake them just above the water. The men nod politely as you pass.

It begins to drizzle, so you all head back to the cabin. There would be no fire outside tonight. Your hosts assemble a fire in the stone fireplace inside. You stay up late again, this time talking about good smells and bad smells as a lazy, drizzly rain scratches at the small windows. Eventually you all retire to your beds—your friends in their rooms and you on the couch again.

A foreign rustle wakes you in the middle of the night. The fire is still simmering, a soft transparent vermilion flickering large shadows on the walls. You open your eyes and lay there and watch the shadows, your eyes getting accustomed to the darkness, the shadows growing lighter and more defined. Suddenly you notice a series of slow movements in the corner. Long, thin shadows slowly twist and shimmy. You sit up a bit and squint to focus your view. Gradually, eventually, the tall, ornate coatrack in the corner begins to turn and spin and move and evolve into a tall, thin man. The man slowly sways and bends, finally filling out, emerging from ornate spindly wood into a man in a tall top hat and evening wear, complete with long black coattails and jaunty bow tie.

The man stretches and undulates as if waking. He turns and notices you. You jump back as the fire snaps and the hard, intermittent rain pecks at the glass. The tall, thin, well-dressed man steps forward in a friendly manner. He steps from the shadows, illuminated by the fire as if entering a cathedral on a sunny spring morning.

He removes his tall stovepipe hat and slowly bends to sit beside you at the end of the couch. He rests the black hat on his lap. He leans forward and utters a forced "Hello," in a slow, cavernous tone.

You try to open your mouth but nothing comes out. So you just smile shyly.

He smiles back in the crisp, amber glow of firelight. He turns his attention to the gentle fire. "It's beautiful," he finally whispers to himself in his deep, gravely voice.

"Yes. It is," you answer in a whisper.

"So, where do you work at night, my dear?" he finally asks.

"I'm . . I'm not from around here," you shake your head, not removing your eyes from the fire.

"Oh," he sighs in disappointment. "I thought I recognized you. I thought you were one of the milk maidens."

And then the men in the mining gear lope past, out of the darkness as if they grew right out of the shadows. Each nods at you silently as they quietly tiptoe their way around the furniture on their way to the door. They walk out into the darkness and you notice the misting drizzle has stopped.

"I'm one of the lighthouse keepers," the well dressed man whispers in his deep pit of a serious voice. "In the daytime I am the coatrack," he returns the top hat to his head. A moment later the top of the hat lights up in a brilliant white.

You gaze at the top of his hat, now a soft glow of fuzzy white.

He just remains there, staring ahead at the dimming fire as if a statue in deep thought. Then he looks at you, tips his hat, nods to you in a slight bow, stands and bids you good night. He turns and disappears into the shadows of the room.

You just sit there watching for a moment. And then you giggle.

strange lights in the clearing

I got home pretty late. The rain was amazing. I'd never driven through anything like that before, like I was driving through an ocean or something—dark water and unusual shapes drifting by as I drove, strange lights worbling and flashing in the distance, distorted by the pouring rain.

I ran inside, from darkness to darkness. No one else was home. They were all up north. I was coming home from the city, off visiting my gal. I walked in and snapped on the light, but nothing happened. The storm must've knocked the power out. I took off my dripping jacket and shoes, hung them in the closet, then walked into the kitchen to call my gal and let her know I had gotten home all right. I picked up the phone but nothing was there. It was silent. And that's when I heard the noises—faint grinding noises out back. I ran down the back hall, past the closet and pantry, to the back door. I looked out, only to see strange lights in the clearing. Murky lights flickered and moved in the rain. Strange lights and shapes in the darkness. Mysterious flashes in the long grass, in the trees, in the mist, in the meadow. My heart raced. What was going on? Shadows and figures slowly lurched in the darkness. It looked like a plane had crashed or something. I ran out in my bare feet, dashing across our backyard to the grassy clearing. Lights swirled and throbbed in the damp fog. Sharp, metallic noises cut the air. I ran and ran. Spots of colored light. Flashes distorted by the mist of rain. Odd noises from the meadow out back.

A mysterious figure walked up to me as I approached. He was tall, with a light in his helmet. "The power's out, son," he shouted through the gusts of wind that deformed the noises. "We're tryin' ta get 'er back. Some trees knocked down the lines. Over there," he nodded over to the clearing.

"Oh, all right," I nodded, looking around. In the distance there were several men in work clothes—dark jump suits and helmets sawing up a tree on the ground with chain saws. The lights on their helmets moved around as they bent and stood and turned and leaned. There were several work trucks parked around the men. Their headlights glowed eerily in the fog and drizzle—orange and red lights on the tops of the cabs swirling and throbbing through thick curtains of rain. From a distance it looked like a plane had crashed, or a spaceship had landed, but they were only utility company workers clearing away a downed tree from the phone and power lines.

"Either way, you should leave," the man leaned closer to me, "The power may not be on for a while. You probably shouldn't stay here tonight." It was difficult to hear him through the droning saws and strong, blowing wind.

I nodded in agreement. "I can go back to the city. The rain seems better now."

"Yeah. Yeah. That would be a good idea. I'm sure you'll be more comfortable there. That's what I'd do. It'd be the smart thing 'cause we're not sure if we have ta re-string this entire line yet. We can't tell what kinda shape she's in. . . You may not have power until . ." he looked back. "Until later tomorrow. . . We don't know just yet."

I nodded, "Yeah, I suppose," and turned and jogged back to the house with my head down. I didn't look back. The rain was lighter now, but still there and blowing all around in the swirling winds.

Once inside, I ran into the bathroom and toweled off. I

thought about changing into dry clothes and heading back into the city, but I was so tired by this time. It had been a long, wild weekend and I just wanted to stay in one place now. I just wanted to be in a quiet place and get some rest. I thought maybe I could go to sleep for a while, then wake up and head back to the city later. The rain might be even lighter then. I knew a lot of people, so finding a couch to crash on for another night wouldn't be a problem.

So I went into my room and crawled into bed. The strange lights flashed and merged on my ceiling and the groaning of saws sputtered faintly—in and out with the rushing wind.

Much later I was awakened by some rustling outside. I figured it was just the work crew packing and driving away or dragging the downed branches. All else was quiet and calm, as if the storm had passed. I heard some people walk past my window in the darkness. They woke me. It seemed like a lot of them, each trudging slowly, as if carrying equipment. "It's all clear," the same man I talked to spoke into a radio.

And his radio answered in a mechanical buzzing and crackling of static: "The landing party at site nine was successful too. Looks like we're all set."

"Good," the man responded as he passed. "The power to this sector is down." Then he added some strange words, but they weren't words really, they were more like sounds—something like: "Klattu idzignat mortu."

The radio hummed and buzzed for a second, and then answered: "Klattu and the others are staged and waiting, so get your troops into position, and stay tuned to coordinate further attacks."

activate the mathias (when in doubt)

I've seen the miracles (just to get that out of the way). You see, I have been able to slow things down. That's why I could see them. I could watch them develop, bloom, and unfold. After I started looking for them, I was able to isolate them so I would know where to look and what to look for. Then I just had to slow myself down so I could really study them.

Once time got slow, I could see the miracles more clearly. Up until then, they were just flashes of instances. But then I figured out a way to slow down time. This enabled me to see the miracles more clearly—so I could read and study them. I think that was one of the problems that people had—all the little miracles would appear and people would only be able to see a bit of them, so preoccupied with other matters or with not knowing where to look to find them. Maybe it would just be a flash of an instance, or maybe life was moving so fast that they would miss the blessed event all together, I don't know. Then an odd thing happened, once I slowed down time and could find and see miracles, I discovered that I could create even more lucky happenstances. I could step in and intercede. I could affect matters. For instance, I could go to a fire and put it out because the fire would be slowed down to nothing, as if slowing a movie to click second by second, frame by frame.

The mathias is the machine that I invented to slow down time. It is a large, electromagnetic device that slows down gravity waves, thus manipulating the time signature around the machine. The alternating currents waft out in pulses. As you adjust the electromagnetic waves, lengths, and duration of the pulses, you then manipulate the speed of gravity, and thus the time around you. I packed the machine into a large panel van. Now I can drive around and affect time within a four block radius. I need to hitch up a large trailer to the truck. The trailer has a big generator inside to power the giant electromagnets that comprise the mathias. I wear a special suit that reverses the polarity of the waves, creating a void around myself, and thus countering the effects of the mathias. So unless you're wearing the special anti-gravitational/magnetic wave suit, or the "magic ice cream suit" as I refer to it, your life will slow drastically—your thoughts, movements, and everything around you will creep to a crawl. But you won't notice this because to you things will be humming along at their standard pace.

I admit that initially when I was fiddling with the magnetic pulses, I was actually trying to open a doorway to some of the other dimensions that I believe are out there waiting to be discovered. I was able to find, isolate, and study atoms, and found that they are so active that they vibrate to such an incredibly fast degree that at every moment they exist in two separate states—vibrating and not-vibrating. And that as they keep vibrating on and off, that time actually splits into two states—the vibrating state and the non-vibrating one. So each state is a possibility. Every moment is divided into two separate possibilities. We exist in one moment, and another version of ourselves exists in that other moment. But the vibrations are so fast and so small that we don't notice them, thus we don't notice the other state, or dimension.

(And since each moment is divided into two separate possible states of existence, each instant after that is then also divided into two more different moments, and these continue to split in half until each possibility is a separate dimension onto itself, although existing and occupying the same physical space. Each parallel possibility is merely a mathematical probability extrapolated out from any occurrence. The more probable or more likely an outcome, the stronger the vibrating waves are, and therefore the closer that possible universe is to you, thus the more likely it is to access and step into. The impossible can't happen, only the most likely of all variables will coalesce and form a possibility. The more likely an event, the more likely those possibilities will group and grow and provide that possibility momentum to build and grow and become a probable reality.

So if each moment exists as two separate possibilities, both in vibration and not in vibration, then each moment after that will also split into two additional possibilities, and each of them will split into two as well, and this splitting will keep growing and growing. The further and further the divide or split grows and develops, the further away each possibility is separated from the others, thus creating several new separate and unique parallel universes of other possible sets of circumstances.

These other possible universes are merely patterns of this—"on, off, on, off," or "off off off on on off off on on on on," etc. until you get a ton of differences in the various possible patterns. Only we can't see the other possible worlds because of how fast the atoms vibrate. But there are other worlds which are all similar but different than our own. And within each event is an on and an off reality, an on and off possibility, each causing slightly different variations and outcomes. As each moment ripples out, there are more and more permeations or possible outcomes, thus forming possible universes, thus more and more possible worlds to slip into)

I thought if I could slow down the vibrations of the atoms, I could open up a rippling magnetic vortex and hop into one of these other possible parallel worlds, by simply turning on or off that world, or those vibrations. I figured I could slow down the atoms by manipulating the gravity waves around us, thus the time around us, thus opening up a little doorway into that next possibility of life, the next mathematical dimension, or probability of events—like holding a mirror up to another mirror and looking into all the possible reflections, as if each were a similar but different world. Anyway, it turns out that I haven't been able to open up a doorway just yet. But the 'slowing down time' thing did work, which is a pretty cool discovery in itself.

So anyway, I go out and field test the entire shebang, by cranking up the voltage and putting on the suit. I go out amongst the populous, observing unnoticed as time is slowed down to where everyone is moving so super slowly that I go unseen. So I can watch things develop at such a slow pace that I can cause change by moving objects around. I can go onto a sports field and alter an error by a sports figure if I want. Or I can cause an error, a slight deviation, by moving a ball ever so slightly so that even in slow motion the camera couldn't pick up the change. I can become the proverbial gremlin in the works. I can bet on a sporting event and then show up, don the magic ice cream suit, enter that event unnoticed, then manipulate the outcome. I can alter elections by changing votes. I can become some of the small miracles of everyday life. I can get you the right poker hand, the right roll of the dice. To a degree I can affect things, change things that are happening around me in real time.

That's how I finance my operation. I have people make bets for me, play poker hands for me, dice games, bowling, pool, you name it. I can affect an outcome by hiding off to the side, hitting a button to activate the mathias and slow down time, and then rush onto the scene to manipulate the pieces. Then I sneak back to my hiding place and reactivate time. So keep on my good side, lest I don the suit and wander into your life, changing things ever so slightly, hiding your keys, messing up your files, changing some numbers, erasing things, reshuffling the deck, affecting the roll of the dice for you.

I still keep fiddling with the mathias, trying to slow things down to an ever more slower and slower pace, still trying to get to the point of being able to spot the vibrations within the on and off status so as to be able to differentiate between the two states, and thus be able to enter that mysterious and alluring other half, the other side. I have a sense that from time to time we can tune into and feel that other side, that we can feel those other possibilities wiggling out there.

I'm also working on several other theories and devices to augment the magic ice cream suit, to try to aid in identifying and splitting the universes. One item is called the "Arabian Avocado," which is a ray gun that changes the path of a moving object ever so slightly, to hold onto or alter the course of a ball or dice from a long distance, so I don't have to walk all the way out onto a playing field and back. This could also hold a falling object in the air until I could fetch a ladder to move said object to safety. Another thought is the "Sly Miss Pendergrass," a hidden earphone connected to all the emergency channels, so I may rush to put out a fire, or rob a bank when the authorities are not close by. This earphone also enables me to hear through walls and spy on specific conversations from great distances, thus enabling me to somewhat know in advance the actions of certain individuals.

Other possible devices and ideas include the "Beckey Anne Myers," a large magnetic ring to hold a specific gravity wave pattern, or doorway, open; and the "Pluto Burrito," a ray that softens a solid so you can walk through it, such as a security door, reinforced wall, or even a bank vault, to enable me to sneak inside of otherwise locked places. And then there's a little something I've got tucked away in my back pocket which I refer to as "The Fendenberg Hypothisis." And, man, she's a real beauty. Or maybe I'll look into a "Mongolian Dangler," or a "Vanilla Henski," or maybe even a "Ricky Blanton" (This last one may enable me to enter previously unknown dimensions and worlds which are not like our own, for instance the squishy land where all the fish-people live. And won't they become just ever so jealous to learn that I have gained access to such technology. Why I bet those fish dudes become just green with envy, or dare I say, greener). But these are just experiments, minor diversions, and past times—just ideas waiting to be developed and improved, just processes and theories, all waiting to be implemented when the time is right. All secrets for now.

In the meantime, I don't really worry about things. The way I figure it, when I'm in doubt, I'll just activate the mathias, and all will be slowed to gorgeous colors, revealing all that could be revealed. And soon I feel all the possibilities will be available to me at any moment—all the mysteries that lay between yesterday and tomorrow. They are all out there, waiting to be inhabited.

the eyes

I rolled out of bed, all groggy hazy fog. I trudged to the bathroom to take my morning pee, my eyes all bleary. As I was washing my hands, my consciousness finally focusing, I got this feeling of things around me—a vague notion of the ceiling (a crack), the floor (a fuzzy line of sunlight from my window beyond), the Miles Davis poster on the wall in my bedroom behind me, the view outside my bedroom window (orange leaves on a branch against a blue sky, puffy clouds)— as if these vivid images were in my mind, as if memories, sharp and alive. I turned and looked around and there they were, just as I pictured in my head. I turned back and looked into the mirror above the sink, and sure enough it looked as though some small eyes had formed on me. Just a curious few. The size of peas. Small ones poking through my skin here and there as if just waking, as if seedlings just beginning to sprout, as if just popping up through the soil. Tiny eyeballs popping through my skin, just the initial signs of things to come.

I went numb. My blood ran cold. There was no feeling. No feeling at all. Nothing in the air. No sound. No sensations whatsoever. I looked all over me, took off my t-shirt, checked myself in the mirror, rubbed some of my tiny new eyes with my finger to see if they were real. They felt harder than I expected. They blinked on their own. And I could sense what they were seeing. In my mind I could feel the images, sense the scenes, see all around, all at once, many different views and perspective coming into consciousness.

I was running late, and thus had to rush to get ready. I threw on a long sleeved turtleneck, embarrassed by my appearance, and yet concerned that the eyes would be sensitive to the sun, because they were so new and all. I covered other parts of myself with a hat and scarf to conceal the several bumps, the several white dots. I figured I could get to the doctor and have them checked out later. Other than the initial shock of the unusual discovery, I actually felt pretty fine.

I got busy that morning, thus couldn't call the doctor. At lunch I sat with some buds. Randy sat down after everyone else. Funny, as he was usually early. He was wearing a long sleeved turtleneck as well.

"Why the long sleeves?" I asked Randy as it wasn't cool out in the least. I thought maybe he had been stricken with the little eyes as well. Maybe it was something going around— something in the food we ate. Some contagion. Some contamination.

Reluctantly, Randy rolled up one of his sleeves.

"My skin seems to be peeling," he announced as he looked his arm over, then laid his arm down on the table before us for all to inspect. "Peeling as if shedding."

We all leaned in, and sure enough, the skin on Randy's arm seemed to be deteriorating.

Joe reached over and tapped his fork on Randy's arm. He poked the side of his fork at it, then rubbed his fork over the deteriorating region, finally raising the fork to pull up and examine under the skin, lifting and looking under a small flap to reveal an emptyish void. We all leaned in. There appeared to be a metallic skeletal structure.

"Looks like a fake arm," Joe muttered as if thinking out loud.

"Bionic," Betsy whispered to herself.

"Gosh," I exhale, "It's like you're really a robot."

"I know," Randy's voice quivered. He retracted his arm. It shook as he rolled up his sleeve and placed his arm on his lap under the table, as if to hide the embarrassing evidence.

"Cool," Joe whispered.

"Do you have super strength?" Dolly's eyebrows raised.

"Let's try to lift things," Miriam smiled.

"No. I don't want to," Randy shook his head.

"You don't ever want to do anything," Dolly scolded.

"Yeah. Can you lift a truck?" Joe asked.

"I don't know," Randy looked down and shook his head.

"Maybe just the front end," Miriam shrugged.

"Maybe it's just the one arm," Betsy returned to her lunch.

"Let's find out," Chester chewed.

"Yeah," Miriam bounced.

"Hey, come on," Dolly looked up at Randy, "Can't you see he's worried."

"I wonder who built you?" Chester looked around.

"Probably your dad," Joe nodded authoritatively.

"Maybe you were a kit. Maybe they ordered you," Betsy reasoned.

"Maybe your parents assembled you," Chester pondered.

"In your basement," Joe nodded.

"Maybe the attic," Dolly thought, "Or the garage."

"Do you remember being assembled?" Miriam looked at Randy.

"Let's take him apart," Chester smiled.

Randy stared, thinking. His shoulders slumped. His head shook slightly, as if in fear. "I don't want to be a robot," he whispered.

"It's probably just the one arm," Betsy shook her head and looked off, as if more concerned about something else entirely.

"Geez," I shook my head, "And here I thought I had problems," I rolled up my sleeve and placed my arm on the table between our lunches. Sure enough, several little eyeballs had forced their way to bulge from my skin. At first the little pea-like eyes just stared blankly. Then some of them began to blink, and then look around. They were a little larger now, but still pretty small as far as eyes go.

"Wow. Eyeballs," Betsy nodded.

"Pretty impressive," Chester leaned in for a gander.

Jeremy leaned in and looked them over. "Like a potato," he whispered.

"Yeah," Joe exhaled, "I get that too." He rolled up his sleeve and placed his arm on the table for all the world to contemplate. Sure enough, he had some larger eyes just randomly scattered on his arm. "Comes and goes," Joe nodded, "Gets pretty bad sometimes." Joe stared down at his arm. The eyes just looked around, some blinking, some bigger than others, some small and lazy.

"Whoa, so that's why they send you to your cousin's sometimes." Betsy nodded.

"Actually, I really stay here," Joe stared at his arm, at his eyes. "My parents just say I'm visiting my cousin's. But really I'm coolin' out," Joe shuddered, his voice cracked, "Ridin' out another outbreak. . ." his voice warbled, ". . My parents don't want to burden the family with our troubles," he trembled.

"Whoa," Chester leaned in, "Those are some peepers."

Joe sighed heavily, wearily, "The eyes. . . The eyeballs. . . They're mine. . . They're my eyes," he swallowed hard.

"How often?" Betsy asked.

Joe swallowed again. "Often enough," he looked away, "I don't want to talk about it."

"No, really," Randy leaned in, "It's starting with this guy," he nodded to me, "Maybe it'll hit the rest of us too."

"This might happen again?" I groaned.

Miriam looked over. "What can they see?"

Joe stared, afraid to speak, as if talking would finally make it real, would announce it to all the world. "Everything," he whispered.

"Wow," Chester exhaled in awe.

"My body betraying me . . . again," Joe gulped.

"Usually, with me, it's my brain," Jeremy looked around.

"With me, it's my mouth," Gus sighed, "That's why I just don't talk no more."

"Sometimes, . ." Joe hesitated, shook his head, looked down, "Sometimes I can see out of them, all of them. . . In my mind I can see all the views at once. Or maybe not see them, maybe only sense them. . . But other times . . . it's like . . . it's . ."

"What?" Betsy whispered.

". . . It's like someone else is controlling them . . . Someone. . . Or some thing," Joe sighed, "Like someone else can sense what I see, what I think."

"Well, who?" Jeremy asked.

"Probably our parents," I sighed. "Who else would bother with us?"

"Maybe one of these creeps around here put a spell on you?" Miriam looked around.

"I bet it's a pill," I stared ahead and nodded, "That's what I figure."

"There goes Margot," Miriam looked far off and sighed, "I bet it's her. I never liked her."

"Why?" I asked, "Where does not liking someone get you?"

"Why?" Miriam looked to me, "Do you like her?"

"Don't really know her," I shrugged, "But I know it's unpractical to dislike someone," I sighed and continued to eat, "How do you know if she ends up getting a job some place you want to work, or knows some interesting people you'd like to meet? Or need to meet. What if she knows someone you'd like to date or something?"

"Ppfffff," Miriam turned away.

"But that's the whole point," I shrugged, "You don't know

what's going to happen. Anything can happen."

"It's all so unstable," Joe stared down and shook his head slightly.

"Well, maybe not 'unstable'," I looked down at my food, then up and all around, "I mean, I guess that's one way to look at it, but there're opportunities out there. . . Just waiting. Why spoil your chances at them? . . . Ignore what isn't necessary. Ignore the veneer, the artifice. . . Look deeper. . . Look for those opportunities."

"Yeah, I agree," Chester nodded, "It's gotta be a pill. To mutate your cells, . . your genes, . . your anatomy."

"Our bodies betraying us again," Miriam clutched her chest.

"Yeah," Dolly nodded, "I bet it's our creepy parents. To keep tabs on us. . ."

"What if they're just trying to help, and it backfired?" Randy sighed, "So we could see more, get smarter, get better grades."

"Yeah, so they can brag to their friends," Jeremy shook his head.

"They only want us to be what they want us to be," Miriam nodded, "Who are they to say what's best for us? Who are they to decide what I want?"

"I bet it's a mutation," Clyde pointed with his spoon.

"Yeah, but what causes it?" Dolly shrugged.

"A pill or elixir that malfunctioned," Clyde looked up in thought, "Went haywire. And now, instead of having increased concentration or hearing or understanding or whatever, you just grow more eyes or something."

"I bet it's something more sinister," Gladys pointed, "An incantation from a sibling or other rival."

"But why?" I asked, amused at the assumptions.

"To get more resources," Gladys shrugged, "Just like always. To elbow us out of the way. To gain favor. Attention. Access. Loot. Whatever. If they can't get ahead through effort, if they can't do it by bad-mouthing, then they might as well pull something like this. . . To bog us down, shove us to the side, keep us hidden away."

"You're just paranoid," I winced, "Just thinkin' too much."

"Am I?" Gladys pondered, "Maybe . . . Maybe. . . But what if? Huh?"

"Meant to slow us down," Dolly nodded, "Burden us with worry. Preoccupy us."

"Maybe it's just stress," Winiferd sighed, "Too many expectations pilin' up. Too much knowledge out there to absorb. It gets to be too much. We fall apart under the weight of it all . . . Our minds revolt."

I shook my head and sighed, "Maybe reasons are futile. Maybe my trip has just begun. Maybe doctors have an answer. Maybe this is all very common, we're just too chicken to expose ourselves to the scrutiny. . . Maybe it's my lot in life not to be afraid. Not to hide. Not to hide it all away. Not to be ashamed."

"Doctors can't help us," moaned Randy.

"I can feel their eyes on me, all over me," I looked around, "The insecure. The haters. The meanies. The ones with nothing better to do. . ."

"Gotta play the cards you're dealt," Gladys whispered to herself.

"What if your cards are all blank?" Winiferd wondered, "What if you're lost in a maze? Blindfolded? Befuddled? Frail and bedazzled?"

"What if, at the end of it all, you're just not lucky? Just don't get the right chances, the chances to improve, to grow," Joe sighed.

Later, we all met up down by the river, on the stone wall at the flower park as always. We sat and talked and thought, watching the leaves drift by, twirling in the air, twisting, turning, sailing, raising, spinning, dancing. We watched the sparkles of sun off the dark blue late afternoon water, the leaves floating past, off to who knows where.

The sun hit the orange and red and yellow trees and the leaves glowed bright orange and lemony yellow, as if lit by a bright light from within, glowing as if bright lanterns in the late day sun.

There were dots in the distance on the long grassy incline up to the road, on the rolling hills, people studying, people out on kind-of dates, people trying to impress other people, people just gathering together for a respite, people just cooling out, cooling that sweet red juice that bubbled and percolated inside.

People appeared here and there in the distance, walking, sitting, lying down, talking, thinking, reading. One of the dark dots grew closer, appearing as a smudge against the yellow fall grass. Maybe it would be someone we knew. Maybe it would turn out to be someone we should know. Maybe it was someone new, a momentary stranger.

"Randy, are you a robot?" Dolly wondered politely, as if concerned.

Randy was silent for a moment, looking down as if stewing. Finally he spoke: "I don't know."

"How can we find out?" Dolly asked, obviously worried.

I wanted to change the subject, so I asked: "I wonder if this one has the eyes?" I nodded over to the approaching stranger. The dark figure appeared to be making a line over to us. "I wonder if he can really see? . . . Or maybe he has the solution to it all."

"Maybe he's the cause of it all," Dolly wondered.

"Too much scrutiny," Jeremy shook his head.

"Soon," I sighed, "There will be no more heroes."

"No more secrets," Winiferd shook her head.

"Too much competition," Wiley looked around, "Too many rivals gunning for you, trying to steal what you've earned, to claim it as their own," she shook her head in confusion and wonder, "This might just be one more phony. One more liar.

One more stealer. . . You can't run down a rumor. You can't beat a lie."

I looked around—at all the deteriorating trees, their leaves leaving them—at all the dots on the grass under the wiry trees. "Feels like they're all watching me," I exhaled, "Their eyes growing on me. Moving all over me."

"That's just the eyeballs," Joe coughed in the wind, "Makes you think differently."

"None of us has control over anything," Dolly stared in thought.

"No one knows what's gonna happen," Chester pondered, then shrugged, "So might as well enjoy the ride."

The dark figure grew ever closer, dressed in a long dark overcoat and long dark scarf, as if to conceal some unreconcilable shame. The figure seemed to lope and twist and sway. Seemed to undulate, and then another appeared in the distance behind the first, again just a smudge in the white and yellow grass, just a smudge fighting the wind and torrent of leaves blowing past.

As the first one grew into view, growing closer, bigger, we noticed he had one gigantic eye. Just a huge, throbbing peeper. Just one big eyeball, the size of a basketball, maybe bigger, but sort of lopsided and drooping, as if half deflated. His other eye seemed normal, maybe smaller than normal. His body bent slightly, perhaps from the strain. But yet he may've just been steadying himself against the wind, the leaves swirling, circling, pelting him as he plowed forward in a beautiful doggedness.

"Gunderson around?" he called through the gusts as he approached.

"Don't know no Gunderson," Dolly called back.

"Auuggghhh," the big eyed figure spat, "Thought he said to meet him 'round here," he stomped the ground and looked about.

"There're other groups around," I nodded.

"Yeah, I been lookin'," the dark figure looked behind himself as he walked. He scanned the distance, his huge eye just a bored glaze. You couldn't help but stare at it in wonder. The hazy eyeball sort of lurched lazily up and off to the side, as if a sad, ineffective mechanism, as if a soggy balloon, just along for the ride.

The second figure caught up to him. This one had several long, whip-like arms which seemed to be covered in wiggling fingers.

The long armed one looked to me. "What's with the eyes?" he asked.

"What's with the arms?" I asked back.

"You tell me," he shrugged, then smiled, "What do you make of 'em?"

"Yeah, that's what I figured," I nodded.

"What's with the big eye?" Miriam asked.

"The better to see you with, my dear," the big eyed guy cooed.

"You lookin' for Gunderson too?" Dolly asked the second one.

"Yeah. And you?" the long armed one nodded, his arms gently undulating at his sides like wet noodles in a bowl of soup.

"Don't know him," Dolly shook her head in the breeze, "Have a seat. Maybe he'll be on by."

"Ah, I don't know," the long armed one stopped a ways from us. He looked around cautiously. "I don't like the water. The last time I was here a group like you tossed me in."

"Well that's not very friendly," Lars turned and looked over.

"Yeah, where does that get you?" Joe sat up.

"What was their mutation?" I asked.

"Yeah," Merideth stared at the ground, "What's their mutation?"

"Yeah," the big eyed dude smiled, "Exactly. What's your mutation?"

"My mutation, your mutation. Blah blah blah," Gus shot, "It's all just one more thing to feel bad about. One more thing to use to try to gain sympathy and favor. One more thing to compare yourself with someone else. One more thing to hold over another person. One more thing to bog us down. One more thing in the way," Gus sighed heavily, "One more thing that just doesn't matter."

A small kid stepped from behind the second one. She looked to be around five. "This is my mutation," she chirped in a little kid voice, "I'm really forty years old."

Miriam looked over. "People should look their age."

"Shut up," the kid squeaked.

"Come on, let's all be nice now," I sighed.

"Hey, I was just sayin' I agree with her," Miriam pointed to the kid.

"Let's go throw rocks at the mimes," Jeremy nodded to a corner of the park.

"We could go to the airport and yell at the airplanes," Chester wiped his eyes.

"Yeah, we could, I guess," Dolly closed her eyes and looked up, letting the warm sun caress her face.

"Like yellin' at jets?" I asked the big eyed fellow.

He sighed and looked at me, "Don't rightly know. Never been out yellin' at jets before." His large, light blue cornea sloshed lazily about in that big deflated white eyeball as if a balloon in a subtle breeze. His other, smaller eye stared ahead, working hard.

"How 'bout you?" I looked down at the kid.

"Yeah, sure," she shrugged, "Sounds like something. . . I like yellin' at stuff."

"Yeah. That's the spirit," I nodded to myself, "Who doesn't?"

"Where did Philomena drift off to?" Dolly looked around, trying to find one of our pals on the horizon, thinking she might be along.

"Haven't seen her in ages," Gus scanned the specs of figures under the huge trees in the grass.

"Prob'ly just busy," Betsy winced in the sun.

"She moved. She's way up in Northeast," Clyde said from below the wall. He was sitting on the ground.

"Yeah, it's probably more of a proximity/availability thing," Gladys nodded.

"Hate that when people drift off," Dolly shook her head, "I don't get that."

The sun was warm, so I removed my turtleneck. "Things change," I commented, forgetting all about my eyes.

"Still," Dolly sighed, "Everything's so fragile. . . Too much change."

"Why do you miss her?" Miriam gestured, "I mean, look around you."

"Yeah, but, . ." Dolly stopped to think a moment, ". . She was nice. Said nice things. Not mean things. . . . . Didn't always try to argue."

"Why would you let people who say mean things try to influence you?" Jeremy wondered, "Why would you ever let them bother you? . . . Who is someone else to say what's right for you?"

"Yeah, whether it's a nice person or a real blue meanie, why would you let another person tell you what to think, what you should be proud of? Or say what's good or what's bad?" Jefferson chucked a rock down to the water, but missed.

Gus whipped a rock down and hit the water with a soft 'ker-plunk'. "Carp are jumpin'," he muttered to himself.

"Gotta think for yourself," Miriam rose and whipped a rock down there, but also missed.

"But still," Dolly rose and dusted herself off, "Guess I just miss her. . . Sometimes it hurts too much to be alive."

"Come on, let's go yell at some airplanes," I stood and took a step, "They ain't gonna yell at themselves, after all."

A few of us slowly slumped from our perches on the old stone wall. Another few were sitting on the ground, leaning against the wall. Some of them peeled themselves from their repose and stumbled to their feet. We said so long to the others who wanted to stay behind. They were not in the mood to yell at airplanes.

We lurched along the water's edge to make our way to the incline below the end of the airport's runways. There was nothing else to do, nothing else available to us.

As we walked the narrow path, we tossed rocks into the water up ahead, trying to hit logs. Then Gus and Chester ran past. They were running in the tall weeds. One of them held up an arm above his head, the other what looked to be a head.

"Whooo hooo," Gus whooped and skipped in celebration.

"Yyyeeeeeee-hhhhhaaaaawwww," Chester called as he shot past, booking around the bend.

Finally Burvin followed with a torso. Randy's torso, with Randy's shirt still on it. The shirt sleeves flopped in the wind above Burvin's head. Then Dolly followed with a leg, trucking with it tucked under her arm as though it were a giant football.

Then we came across another crumbling old stone wall. Several middle-aged men were sitting on it, just staring off into the distance. You could tell they had no jobs. You could read it in their faces, see it in their eyes. It was as if they knew their lives were slipping away, going to waste, their chance at a chance dwindling with every breath. We nodded as we passed and they nodded in return. They sat as if waiting, waiting for something to come along, to inspire them, bite them in the behind, give them a reason, give them a chance. There sat a whole line of them. I could see them all now, with all my many eyes.

It got me to thinking—that maybe I shouldn't let my new eyes go to waste, that I shouldn't let my gifts go to spoil. And so I made a deal with myself, that I'd try not to let the day slip away from me, that I'd try not to let the day go to waste.

And now I feel that I am to bear witness to this notion. Suddenly I saw things more clearly and from several angles—that it was my mission to impart this to you, to bear witness to the waste.

I found them in the weeds
behind the barn

Whipping sheets of wind swirl waves of chalky dust around me. I stare off into the distance. Nothing moves out here but the long, swaying grass and the curtains of dust—not the line of trees draped across the rolling fields, not the flat clouds that hang on the hazy horizon. No, they're all too tired or hot to do anything but just sit there. It looks like me and the clouds will be stuck out here in another uneventful summer, stuck out here in the middle of nowhere again, together on the hot and dry farm.

I walk back in from the fields for lunch. I decide to take a shortcut by hopping over a fence and walking through a patch of sand and weeds behind the barn. My boot happens to catch something, sort of tripping me up for a second. I stumble a little and turn around, thinking I hit an old root or rock or fence post or something. I step back and gaze down, and there, protruding out of the sand, is a shiny arc of metal. I bend to investigate as I don't want any metal shards messing with the tractor tires.

I dig around in the white sand and long weeds, finally pulling out the curving piece of metal. I raise it and examine it. It looks like the clasp of a helmet ring that snaps a helmet to a flight suit. It coulda been here for years. I stand and kick around in the sand some more and pretty soon I hit another something—something big. I drop to all fours and begin digging with my hands, finally uncovering another curving, shiny, thin piece of metal. This one is quite large. I tug and tug, gradually working it free and pulling it to the surface. It's the size of a car door, but very light. It's a bright, shiny silver, but covered in dust from the ground. It's slippery to the touch and almost mirror-like. It too must've been buried for years. I push more sand around and find another arching silver chunk protruding from the ground. This one is dull and dusty, obscured in the sand by the tall weeds and grass. The silver metal has faint markings in reds and whites—weird marks, like letters, but in a language I've never seen before. I dig and dig, finally pulling up the second large piece—again the size of a car door, but very very light. I set it aside and kneel to think for a moment. Finally, I lean both of them against the barn and run around to get a shovel, hoping to find more.

They are like pieces of an aircraft or something—like one of those shiny silver jets from the early 1950s. Then, in digging around in the sand and grass, I find a weird pair of sunglasses. They're like a wrap-around plastic visor, only very thin and narrow. They're gray with dust, almost invisible, buried under days and years of blowing sand. They look old, like from the early 1970s, like those little dark plastic wrap-around jobbies that really super cool guys like rock stars and Richard Petty and Steve McQueen would wear. I brush them off, thinking, hey great, new wrap-around sunglasses. Then I try them on, to see how they fit. They're snug. I feel their warmth tightly on my face. At first it seems like they're warm from being out in the sun in the hot sand and weeds. But then I get to thinking that it's as if they're mechanical somehow, an electrical kind of warmth, a thick kind of warmth. "They're body-heat activated," a voice suddenly appears in my head as if remembering from an old, distant dream.

I look around in them. Everything is dark, but sure enough,

in a second or two, things get lighter, the fields coming into view, clearer and clearer with each breath. They shade the sun perfectly. And then tiny lights begin fluttering in the lenses. But it isn't like they are right there, all big and blobby in front of my eyes. No. It's like the lights are way off in the distance.

The lights begin to twinkle and then string together, forming words way out there: The temperature, the distances of objects; the trees, the blowing grass, the tractor, the hay barn, the silo. Then one big line flashes in blue: "Welcome back, Captain Fjoorjbjoorj, we missed you." Then another little message appears in lights up in the corner, way out there in the sky above the field. The message reads: "For further instructions, pinch your left earlobe."

I pinch my left earlobe and sure enough, a faint voice appears in my ear. At first it's just a humming buzz, but soon it gathers itself into a string of static, and then garbled gibberish. It sounds like a recording, like the faint fuzz of a radio signal. And then, through the rough sizzle of static, the words begin to slow and even out. "Welcome back, . . . Captain Fjoorjbjoorj, we've been waiting for you. We've missed you so. . ." The slight mechanical whisper crackles in a static wobble—fast and slow, fast and slow, as if being beamed from the other side of the universe. "We've dispatched a rescue team to retrieve you directly. Your assistance is needed desperately. . ."

the golden eagle of montenegro

A little boy is sleeping soundly, the city around him encased in a deep blanket of winter. The moonlight is glistening off the pale blue snow as small shadows creep along the sides of the house, scampering fast and low. Next thing you know they are inside, sneaking down the hallway and infesting the vents and ducts. It is only a matter of time now.

The little boy awakens to a series of scratching sounds. He shakes his head slowly and gradually rises from his pillow. An odd greenish light pops on him in the darkness and he is face to face with a strange goblin-like man. The small creature is crouching at the side of the bed, his pointed ears pull back and twitch, pellets of ice entwine in his pointy little beard. "Where is it?" the creature whispers. His unearthly voice is deep and growly. "Where is it?" the goblin clutches a small lantern, raising it to light the night air.

The little boy shakes his head. He figures he is dreaming. "It's up your nose, you ugly goatsucker. Now leave me alone," the boy mumbles through sleepy, half open eyes, then his head falls back onto his pillow.

"Whheeerrrreeee iiissssss iiiitttt," the goblin-man hisses and shakes the misty green light across the boy's face. He extends his stubby arm closer to the boy. Several short shadows bob and sway in the darkness, sticking close to the walls. The shadowy figures grunt and breathe heavily as hissing noises whistle through their noses. Some of them pant and growl and drool, "Eeeerrrrrrrrrhhhhh . . . Gggggrrrrrrrrrrrrrrrrrrr."

"We've come for The Golden Eagle of Montenegro. Now hand it over," the goblin insists, his red eyes narrowing, his brow furrowing.

The boy opens his eyes and watches the small, hairy man for a moment. As his eyes adjust to the light, he begins to notice the creature's features, the green light above reflecting a grotesque elfin figure with a narrow nose and long scraggly hair. The creature's face is short and wide, big mouth, missing teeth and yellow fangs, hot breath, stubbly beard, warts and bumps, wrinkly gray skin, wrapped in a dark tattered wool overcoat with a hood and long scarf.

"The Eagle of Montenegro. Now," the small man insists.

"The what?" the boy lowers his brow in confusion.

Then a different deep gravely voice growls in the distance, "You know what we're here for, now hand it over."

"Yeah," another joins in. "And we mean business."

"I'm about to rip your esophagus out with my teeth," the first one adds.

"Listen, guys, I don't have any gold. You must have the wrong house," the boy explains, still lying down, glowing in the weak green misty specter of faint light. "I . . I don't have any gold. And I certainly don't have any golden eagle. . . And neither does my dad. He . . He sells insurance. Do you need any coverage?"

"Hand it over, little boy," the first one continues, "and we'll spare your life."

"You wouldn't want us to slit your belly open. To spill your guts. To gut you like a fish," a glint of steel flashes in the corner.

"Listen . . . Listen guys, I appreciate you being threatening and all, but I just don't have any gold. Honest. I . . ."

"You took it from us, now give it back. It's rightly ours," one mumbles in the darkness beyond. "We need it."

"Give it back, little scoundrel," another growls from the shadows. "It is ours."

"Yeah, we stole it fair and square from the Lumpers, then you stumbled across it in the woods while camping with your family last summer and took it from us. Return it at once," another demands. "It belongs to us."

"Look, I can see you're upset. You can look around if you'd like. All I got is an old Playboy at the bottom of my pajama drawer over there," the boy points, "But that's about it. I found that in a garbage can down the block. You can have it if you'd like."

"Hand over The Eagle of Montenegro and we'll spare your parents," one huffs from the shadows.

"Listen. . . Listen guys. You can have my sister. Take her. Please . . . Really. She's yours. She's right down the hall," the boy whispers so as to not wake anyone. "But. . . But once you take 'er, you . . . You gotta keep her, o.k? I mean, fair is fair."

"No little girls," the first one jiggles the little lantern impatiently, "Just the gold."

"Look guys . . . Guys, if I had any gold do you really think I'd be living here? Huh? In my parents house? In this house. Here?" the boy sits up. "Naw, man. Not me. I'd buy Yankee stadium, man. Now there's a class-A crash pad, man."

"Listen Billy, we know you got it hidden here somewhere and we're prepared to rip this place apart. Now do you really want that? Huh? Think of the mess that would cause for you. You really wanna be cleanin' up the rest of the month?"

"Yeah. Just hand it over and save us all a lot of hassle and a big grizzly mess for ya'll. You know, guts and limbs everywhere. Entrails hanging from stuff. Pools of innards. That sort of thing."

"We've already ransacked your tree house, Billy."

"And your fort in the gully out back. The one down behind the woodpile on the other side of the garage, Billy. Now listen and listen good . . ."

"Billy? Why you keep callin' me Billy? Huh? Do I look like a Billy to you?" the little boy points. "Huh?"

"You're Billy Cheever, aren't you? This is the Cheever residence, yeah?"

"No. No. I'm Darren. Darren Spahalla," the boy explains.

The first gremlin's head snaps back. He gazes down at the boy for a moment, then looks back to the shadows. "Darren?" The rest shrug. The first one looks back over to the boy. "Oh, sorry. We must have the wrong house."

"Yeah, sorry kid."

The boy nods in understanding, "Yeah. All right. Don't worry about it guys."

"Sorry for waking you," one gestures from the shadows. "Good night. Sleep well."

"We musta gotten our directions mixed up. We're not from around here."

"No problem. It happens," the boy nods as if really bored by the entire situation.

"Back to bed now," the first goblin reaches out his claw and places it on the boy's head and pats it down. The weird green glow snaps off. "Back to sleep, you."

Several of the hunched-over shadows waddle out. "We'll try ta make it up ta ya some day, kiddo."

"Yeah. Yeah. Sure thing."

"Really?" the boy considers this prospect in the darkness, "'Cause there's this real jerk, Pete Morris, who lives down the block. 3381 James Avenue. An' he's always hasslin' everyone."

The first one turns around in the doorway, his shadow hunched and leaning to listen.

"The purple house at the end of the block. Kitty-corner from the gas station. Down there," the boy gestures his arm. "Yeah, he's a real piece of work. If it wouldn't be too much trouble he could use a good whoopin'. It'd really be a big help. Save people a lot of trouble in the long run. . . If it wouldn't be too much trouble, that is. I mean, while you're still in the neighborhood and all. Maybe you could all pay him a little visit. Flare your nostrils and all that. Scare the livin' daylights outta him. Throw a good scare into him. Straighten him out. He's really got it comin'."

"Yeah, sure thing, kid. Will do."

"Yeah. No problem. 3381. Last purple house 'till the gas station."

And with that the strange, lumpy shadows were gone, and the boy settles deeper into his warm bed, the crisp wind blowing outside. He hugs his teddy bear under the covers, tightly clutching The Golden Eagle of Montenegro hidden safely inside of it.

the sandbox

My little niece, Tatiana, and I are playing in her sandbox. It is a very old sandbox, melting into the corner of her backyard, slowly spreading over the years to disappear into the grass, as if to run away from itself—sand and dying grass everywhere, all but indistinguishable from the corner of yard now.

The yard has crept into it over time and the sand has leaked out, each growing to mix into one another—sparse tuffs of invading grass and sand moving into dry patches—so as to look like the remnants of a long lost beach. The wood on the sides of the sandbox are rotting terribly and have sunk into the yard and spread far apart. They now lay at least twenty feet from one another. We sit in the shade, under a twisting, leaning, old gray tree that sags limply, slowly sinking into the corner of the yard, lower and lower with each passing year, down into the sand and patches of dry, yellow grass.

Suddenly my little niece digs up a very large bone. It is long and thin and white. "Hey, what's this?" she squeaks, slowly looking it over. My head snaps up from my digging. She lays it down and starts to use it as a plow, gently relocating grains of sparkling sand, pushing and evening out a spread. Then she pokes down into another bone. She reaches into the sand and pulls up another one. Now I am confused. "Where'd all these bones come from?" I ask. "I don't know," she slowly sings without looking up, still dragging the second bone to form a line in the dry sand. "Hhhmmm, maybe a dog buried them?" I wonder as I pat some sand. She holds out the second bone. It looks like a femur. "Or maybe it's an old dog—buried in the back yard a hundred years ago, long since forgotten?" I question.

Then I hit something hard. I reach further into the sand and dig around. Gripping something odd, I pull up a skull. An old skull. "Haw," Tatiana squeals at my discovery, as if I just pulled a rabbit from a hat, but then kids are always impressed with free stuff. "A real dilly," I say, brushing sand from its brow, lifting it to gain a closer view. "Boy, this one sure got himself into a pickle," I exclaim, looking over the old skull. "Why just look at the size of the hole in this guy's head," I poke my finger in a quarter-sized hole in the top of the skull and feel around. I set it aside and reach into the sand, plunging deeper with both hands. The sand is thick and warm and grainy. I lean my way in until I hit something hard. I feel around, grab onto a stick or something, and work it to the surface. I tug up a skeletal arm and shoulder. I lift it out and set it aside, sand dripping from it. I examine it for a moment, looking it over, then I reach in again and feel around. This time I bring up a full skeletal rib cage connected to a part of a spine. I set that one aside too. My little niece claps at this. "Yeah," she beams. "Another one!"

They're sun bleached white bones. "Whhoooo, must be a hundred years old, maybe more. Maybe five hundred," I whistle. Tatiana pounds her two bones against the sand like drumsticks. "Yeah!" she says. I reach in again, my hands disappearing deeper and deeper, all the way down to my elbows this time. I feel something hard and solid, wiggle my arms around to gauge its size. Finally I get a handle on it and, grunting, I slowly work it up, moving it from side to side to raise it. It is big and solid and thick and heavy. I lift and pull and tug to get it free. It is a little wooden chest—built solid and heavy. With both hands I drag it out of the sand by its handle. I set it aside, brush it off, and look it over.

It has metal latches and leather straps and a big ol' padlock. I look over at the arm I found—pure white bones and complicated hand lying in the dry, sandy grass. And sure enough, clutched in the hand, nestled in the web of delicate thin bone, is a rusted metal key, long and brown. I pry the key from the nest of thin white bone and fit it into the lock and open the lid. My niece sits up and peers over to catch the sun glinting off a mound of shining coins—silver and gold, and sparkling jewels of every color piled inside. She sits back and smiles and claps some more. "Yeah," she beams and claps, "Now we can buy a monkey!"

ABOUT THE AUTHOR

Tony Rauch lives in Minneapolis, Minnesota. He is a Senior Project Designer and Urban Designer at an architecture firm. His books include *Laredo* (Eraserhead Press), *I'm right here* (Spout Press), and several forthcoming titles. Visit him online at www.trauch.wordpress.com.

www.ingramcontent.com/pod-product-compliance
Lightning Source LLC
Chambersburg PA
CBHW020343260626
47156CB00004B/1669